So the knockout drops had been meant for me

How was I supposed to avoid disaster if two of these men were willing to go to such lengths to get rid of Carrie? Either I stayed in character and let it happen, or I betrayed the trust of a client and defended myself. Assuming I could decide which of my male pursuers had murder up their sleeves.

I turned away from the window, filled with the most peculiar feeling. I'd never worried about being alone with a man, knowing that nothing would happen that I couldn't handle. Now I was virtually alone with three men, and had no idea which way to turn.

The dim parlor wasn't soothing or romantic. It was a lair for the spider who was pulling me into his web.

ABOUT THE AUTHOR

Sharon Green is a well-known science-fiction author. She loves to write stories with a special twist, and in *Fantasy Man* she provides her readers with an added twist. Sharon makes her home in Nashville.

Books by Sharon Green

HARLEQUIN INTRIGUE

152–HAUNTED HOUSE
224–WEREWOLF MOON

Fantasy Man

Sharon Green

Harlequin Books

TORONTO • NEW YORK • LONDON
AMSTERDAM • PARIS • SYDNEY • HAMBURG
STOCKHOLM • ATHENS • TOKYO • MILAN
MADRID • WARSAW • BUDAPEST • AUCKLAND

Harlequin Intrigue edition published September 1993

ISBN 0-373-22244-0

FANTASY MAN

Printed in U.S.A.

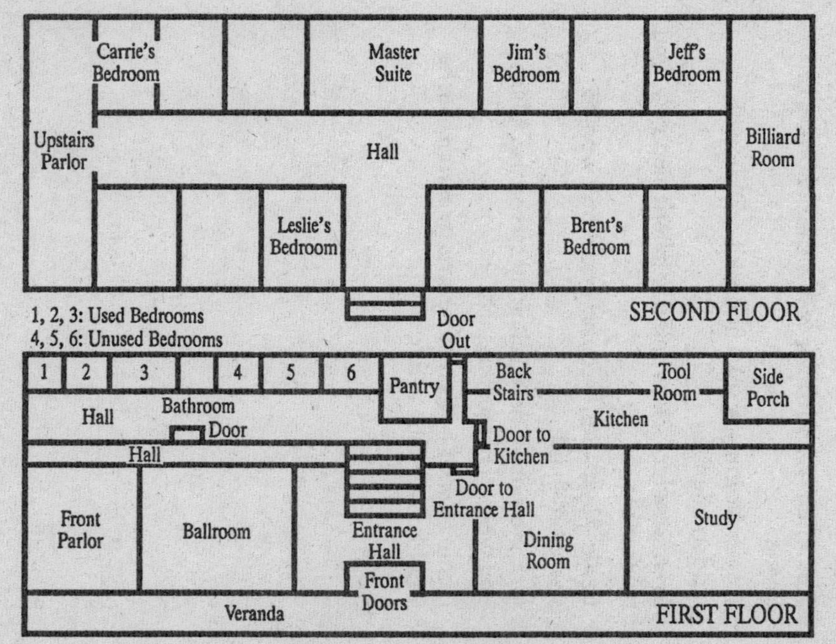
Carrie's Bedroom
Master Suite
Jim's Bedroom
Jeff's Bedroom
Upstairs Parlor
Hall
Billiard Room
Leslie's Bedroom
Brent's Bedroom
SECOND FLOOR
1, 2, 3: Used Bedrooms
4, 5, 6: Unused Bedrooms
Door Out
1
2
3
4
5
6
Pantry
Back Stairs
Tool Room
Side Porch
Hall
Bathroom
Door
Kitchen
Door to Kitchen
Hall
Door to Entrance Hall
Front Parlor
Ballroom
Entrance Hall
Dining Room
Study
Front Doors
Veranda
FIRST FLOOR

CAST OF CHARACTERS

Ann Mellion—Her job was turning into a deadly affair.

Jeff Allyn—A bachelor with a special brand of loving.

James Nolan—A sexy financial adviser with hidden talents.

Brent Lawler—He wanted to inherit money . . . and much more.

Leslie Allyn—Jeff's cousin who didn't want to share anything.

Mrs. Haines—She'd faithfully served the Allyns and wanted her just deserts.

Danie Haines—His mother was a servant, but he would never take orders.

Prologue

In the wintry Washington, D.C., night, a dark form moved through the deserted neighborhood of warehouses, every once in a while checking casually to make sure no one was following. The man had parked half a dozen blocks away despite the wind and cold, clearly preferring to walk. When he reached the door to one of the warehouses, he paused for a final look around before going in.

Beside the warehouse, a woman laughed softly to herself, then slipped in another door she had had time to open before the man had appeared. The building was only a little warmer than outside, but Ann Mellion was glad to be out of the wind. What made her even happier, though, was the background check she'd done on the man she'd followed there. Knowing of his ownership of this unused warehouse had let her get in there ahead of him.

Dressed in dark clothes, Ann slipped silently from aisle to aisle in the dim warehouse. Tall, blond, and in her mid-twenties, she was an experienced investigator for the firm of Chandler and Rich. Influential residents of D.C. often used Chandler and Rich when they had a problem that needed to be kept confidential.

That was the reason Ann was there—to follow a man who had been blackmailing the firm's newest client. Her first objective was to find and destroy the evidence the client was being blackmailed with. After that they could discuss having the man charged in a court of law.

Ann could feel the heavy silence all around her, interrupted only by the murmur of voices somewhere ahead. As she'd suspected, her quarry *was* meeting someone here, and hadn't come to the warehouse simply to check his files.

It was another couple of minutes before Ann got close enough to those speaking to understand what was being said. The man she'd followed had reached a group of five others only a moment or two earlier and was demanding to know what was going on. Ann settled herself behind some boxes in the shadows and listened.

"...insisted on meeting you face-to-face," one of the men was saying to her quarry.

A typical heavy with delusions of authority, Ann decided, seeing the annoyance in the man's expression.

"And why should a meeting like this be necessary?" the warehouse owner countered, looking only at an older man who stood among the rest. He was tall and gray haired and slightly stooped, giving Ann the impression of mildness of character. He all but quavered, which her quarry seemed to enjoy seeing.

"My dear sir, consider what you've asked me to do," the older man protested, his voice frail and unsteady. "If I'm to sell my honor, at the very least I am entitled to meet the man who buys it. And perhaps even dissuade him from insisting on the purchase."

"Surely you're not thinking of trying to back out?" the blackmailer said, his words too smooth to hold genuine surprise. "We discussed this, and you agreed that you would prefer to copy those files for us rather than have the world find out about your little... hobbies. Have you changed your mind? If so, the tapes can be in the hands of the press by tomorrow morning—"

"No!" the older man exclaimed, then softened his tone. "No, those tapes must be given to no one but me. But the price you ask...can't it be something that *isn't* top secret? There are many files in my care, and some of them won't be released for years to come. Surely something like them would—"

"Would be worth less than the film used to copy them," Ann's quarry interrupted flatly. "What I want are those designs, and you'll bring the first of them tomorrow night. Won't you."

"Very well," the older man conceded in defeat. He hadn't been asked; he'd been ordered. "I'll bring the first of the designs tomorrow night, but I must insist that you be here personally to receive them. I won't leave them with a careless underling, then be accused of not having brought them at all."

"Why would you worry about something like that?" the first man who had spoken demanded. Ann's quarry had been about to agree to the condition, but the first man's annoyance had interfered. "If you gave the designs to me and I lost them, the boss would know. And why couldn't you just go back and make another copy?"

"It—it would be dangerous to have to go back again," the older man said. The explanation sounded smooth enough, but the words had been spoken a little too fast. "And I meant no insult to you, sir. It was an incompetent underling I had in mind, which you certainly are not."

"You better believe I'm not," the man growled, his anger having grown at the apology rather than being soothed. "I'm not so dim that I don't know a con when I see one. If you want the boss here when you deliver, chances are you're going to deliver something besides plans. What have you got in mind, huh, old man? Thinking about bringing the cops?"

He reached into his coat, most likely going after a gun. The three men who hadn't spoken were staring at the older man, their expressions hard and unyielding. Even Ann's quarry was looking suspicious, which meant it was about to be all over for the poor guy. The old man himself seemed to realize the game was up, and that was the instant he moved.

With surprising strength, he grabbed one of the surrounding men by the coat, threw him into the others, then took off for the closest aisle.

"Some old man!" Ann murmured.

He moved like a young man in excellent shape now, but he still didn't have much of a chance. Two men who hadn't gotten tangled up with the one he'd thrown produced guns that would stop him before he reached safety.

Under normal circumstances, Ann would have thought twice about bringing up the gun she carried. Chandler and Rich frowned on their representatives going around shooting people and she wasn't a hothead, but a man's life was at stake. Ann's weapon was already in her hand, and before either of the two men could shoot, she aimed and fired.

One of the men shouted in pain and dropped his gun. Shooting the first man also distracted the second. Instead of firing at the fugitive, he turned and fired in her direction, then everyone was running for cover.

The next few minutes saw a lot of rounds being exchanged. Ann carefully picked her shots. There was only one more clip besides the one already in her automatic. She was having very little trouble keeping opponents at bay, but this wasn't something that would last. All they had to do was slip around behind her....

Suddenly, Ann heard the sound of doors being broken in, and a third side was added to the shootout. "Federal agents! Throw down your weapons!" the newcomers yelled.

But Ann's opponents didn't obey. Instead they began to fire at the feds, which was a definite mistake. The agents were armed with heavy riot guns, and their sound was almost deafening as it echoed through the warehouse. One of the blackmailer's men screamed as he fell, shot down from where he'd been kneeling, and that seemed to do it. The others gave up, including Ann's quarry.

The federal agents spread out quickly to cover the surrendering gunmen, then began cuffing them. Others began to search the warehouse, and Ann discovered what they were looking for when they spotted her. When they trained their weapons on her, she lost no time in raising her arms to surrender.

"Take it easy, boys. I'm on your side," Ann said, standing and moving forward as ordered. "I'm also here on business, which I can prove. I have ID in my jacket."

"Save it for Elliott," the agent who took her gun advised. "He's the one who'll be asking the questions, so keep your answers for him. And hope he believes them."

Which wasn't too likely, Ann surmised as the agent turned her around and cuffed her wrists. She was annoyed with herself for walking into the middle of a covert operation, but she really hadn't had much choice. If she'd known, she would have quickly gone the other way....

But then their inside man would now be dead. As she was led toward the larger group of men, Ann looked toward the aisle the erstwhile "old man" had run into. It took a lot of courage to act as bait in one of those operations, especially when your backup was outside. Ann wondered what the man really looked like, and whether he was all right.

"Okay, now where do *you* fit in to all this?" a voice asked, catching Ann's attention. The agent who approached her had the name Elliott stitched into the breast of his jacket.

"I'm Ann Mellion. I work for Chandler and Rich," Ann responded. "I was assigned to follow that blond man over there in an effort to recover something he took from one of our clients. I have identification inside my jacket, and my boss's name is Miller Houston. You can check with him to verify what I'm saying. Messing up a federal operation is a definite no-no at Chandler and Rich—Miller will probably kill me."

"He may have to stand in line," Elliott said with a faint smile, reaching for Ann's jacket. "Being here doesn't put you in a very good light, Miss, no matter who you work for. Let's—"

Elliott cut his own words short as his hand went to his ear, and only then did Ann notice the button receiver he wore. He listened intently and, after a couple of minutes, grunted as though in agreement. Then he gestured to the agent who had handcuffed Ann.

"Let's have the key, Reynolds," he called, looking at Ann with more of a smile. "I understand we have something to thank you for, Ms. Mellion. That was a brave thing you did. Drawing fire to let our man find cover saved his life, and I'd like to add our thanks to his."

"He's coming over to thank me?" Ann asked, looking again toward the aisle where the man had disappeared. "That isn't really necessary."

"No, I'm sorry, he won't be coming over," Elliott said as the cuffs were removed from Ann's wrists. "He's an undercover specialist, and most of *us* haven't seen him without that disguise. I'm sure he'd like to thank you personally, but you'll just have to settle for getting the words secondhand from me. You understand, I'm sure."

"Certainly," Ann agreed, swallowing the disappointment she felt. A man like that, who risked his life for his country on a regular basis... She'd never met a man like that, and part of her had been hoping...well, so much for fantasies.

"Would I be stepping on your toes again if I asked for the chance to take a look at the warehouse office?" Ann asked Elliott with a sigh that put dreaming aside. "I still need to recover what that man took from my client and, hopefully, keep it confidential. If that would interfere with your investigation too much—"

"Ms. Mellion, we owe you," Elliott interrupted. "I'll send Pollard to keep you company, but if you find what you're looking for, you're welcome to it. From what we hear, there will be plenty left for us to use. Hey, Pollard, over here!"

Agent Pollard went with Ann to look for the office, and once inside they searched until they found hidden and well-locked files. Pollard took only a few minutes to open the locks, showing one of the reasons Elliott had sent him with her. The second reason came clear once Ann had removed the file she needed; Pollard stood himself in front of the rest, grinning faintly. Ann now had all she was going to get, and if she misunderstood that there would be trouble.

But Ann already had what she wanted, so she thanked Pollard and began to make her way out of the warehouse. Well, she had almost all of what she wanted, but a certain introduction was specifically *not* part of the deal. Ann went back to work, intending to forget the incident, but the next day flowers and a card were delivered to her office. . . .

Chapter One

It was a pretty day for a Tuesday, about as bright and fresh as D.C. gets in late spring. It was also just past rush hour, which meant that the volume of traffic was a shade less than overwhelming. The taxi I took actually got me within a block of the Madison Building before becoming hopelessly snarled in an ocean of honking motionlessness.

Leaning forward, I handed the driver a ten-dollar bill. "Keep the change, and I'll walk from here."

"Are you sure you know where it is?" the man asked anxiously, taking the money absently while casting a dirty look at the traffic ahead. "A girl like you shouldn't be walking around this town alone. I have a daughter about your age. What if I turn off the meter and the rest of the trip is on me?"

"That's very nice of you, but I'm already late," I told him gently with a matching smile. "And I'll be just fine. I know this neighborhood, and I can take care of myself. Have a really nice day."

He tried arguing a bit more, but my getting out of the cab and walking away with a wave ended the discussion. A couple of years earlier, I would have told the man exactly how old I was and exactly how well I could take care of myself. It wouldn't have done any good, but I still would have blamed him for his concern.

As I made my way along the sidewalk with the remnants of the early-morning crowd, I smiled faintly to myself. So what if I was twenty-six but looked about seventeen? Wasn't it an incredible asset in my work? My pale-blond hair and blue eyes made me appear not only young but innocent and vulnerable.

"Sure," I muttered with a sigh. It was a great help to my work. It was just my personal life that it didn't do much for. How could you find a man, when all you attracted were boys?

"Hey, Tommy!" I heard, then Ron Ford caught up to me. "First day back from assignment?" he asked with a grin. "Me, too. Let's have dinner tonight and swap war stories."

"The last time I had dinner with you, it was war without the stories," I reminded him. "I'm not in the mood for another wrestling match, so let's just forget it. And don't call me 'Tommy.' "

"Why not?" he asked with the same grin. "Everybody else does, and somehow it fits better than Ann. Come on, have dinner with me. I promise I'll be a perfect gentleman."

"Sure you will," I responded with a snort. Ron was a good example of just how handsome a man with brown hair and eyes could be, but I'd learned the hard way how heavily he relied on his good looks. Rather than asking, he tended to simply help himself, certain that he was too attractive for any woman to refuse. I'd done a little more than refuse, which was why I couldn't understand his coming back a second time.

"Are you saying you don't think I know *how* to be a gentleman?" he demanded, supposedly hurt. "Okay, I made a mistake last time, and I'm a big enough person to admit it. If you'll do the same, we can forget about bygones and think only of the future."

"What mistake did *I* make?" I asked, really curious. We'd reached the Madison Building by then, and I stopped to let Ron open the door. "If you're suggesting I should have *broken* your arm instead of just spraining it..."

"Come on, we both know you caught me by surprise," he said with a laugh of dismissal as he followed me inside. "No, your mistake was in letting nervousness get the best of you. You didn't stop to remember that I have too much experience with women to hurt one, especially one who looks like you."

At that point I could all but feel his eyes moving over me, taking in the cream-and-tan suit I wore. The knit blouse showed off my breasts, the short skirt showed off my legs, and Ron's last statement showed what an imbecile he was.

"But I wasn't worried about being hurt," I told him, annoyed. "I was just remembering what I'd heard around the office about you. I can understand practicing something until you get it right, Ron, but the general opinion is that you're practicing the wrong thing."

"What's that supposed to mean?" he demanded, this time without any sort of amusement. He stopped short just outside the elevator, but I continued on in before turning to smile at him.

"It means that you're a dud in bed," I told him. "That's dud, not stud, and I don't enjoy being bored.

Why don't you find an inexperienced girl to be that perfect gentleman with?"

His face darkened with humiliation, then it disappeared behind the closing elevator doors. Part of me wanted to be ashamed for saying that to him, but the rest understood too well what he'd been trying to do. Ron had wanted to take advantage of someone who was young and innocent, just as he had already done with a number of girls in our office. Some of them hadn't minded, but the others...

The others had thought there was something wrong with *them* when he didn't call again. His victims didn't seem to understand it was a little boy they were dealing with, one who lost interest as soon as he had what he wanted. A little boy in a man's body, who never saw the woman inside the physical appearance.

The elevator dinged to announce the sixteenth floor. The double doors of the office were directly opposite the elevator, raised gold letters on dark wood announcing Chandler and Rich in a boldly discreet way. Nothing in the way of elaboration was written below, which most people considered very impressive. If you didn't know what Chandler and Rich did, you had no business calling there.

Inside the double doors was the tastefully furnished reception area. Carol looked up when I walked in. Her dark hair was neatly arranged as usual, her suit impeccably tailored and her smile as formal as a butler's. It warmed a little when she saw me, and she nodded as I passed. I returned the smile while ignoring the four people waiting separately for their appointment times, and headed on back to my office.

"Ann, welcome back," Marsha said from her desk. "Are you all finished with the assignment?"

"After two weeks, I damned well better be," I told her with a smile. "Could I impose on you for a cup of coffee? This may be Tuesday, but to me it feels like a Monday."

"Oh, you poor thing," she commiserated with a chuckle. "Go sit down and I'll bring it right in."

She handed me my mail before heading for the coffee room, and I glanced through it while standing there. Marsha had already taken care of most of it, proving again what a lifesaver she was. I shared her with three other field operatives, but the way she handled our business made each of us feel she worked for us alone. If we ever had to get along without her...

"Hi, Tommy," Ray Wise said as he passed on the way to his office. "How's it going?"

"Swimmingly, Wise, just swimmingly," I answered without looking up. "And the next time you call me that, I'll call your wife and tell her you've been arrested for indecent exposure. If she doesn't fall down laughing, you'll spend a month explaining it away."

"Vindictiveness doesn't suit you, Tommy," he answered without looking back. "Besides, my wife is at her mother's. Have a nice day."

I glanced at his retreating back and shook my head. I'd forgotten that threats didn't bother Ray, which was one of the things that made him such a good field operative. Past middle age, pudgy and balding, he nevertheless managed to rack up a lot of successfully completed assignments. If Ron hadn't gotten to me, I never would have noticed *what* Ray was calling me. Maybe what I needed was a vacation.

"Here's your coffee, Ann," Marsha said with a smile as she returned. "I'll carry it into your office for you."

Without waiting for an answer she headed for my office, her short, round body moving with brisk efficiency. I raised my brows before following, wondering what was going on in that red-haired head. Marsha knew I was capable of carrying a cup all by myself, so why was she—

The answer came as soon as I reached the doorway, and I stopped short to stare. The bouquet of flowers sitting on my desk was beautiful, but it really shouldn't have been there. Not on my first day back. . . .

"What's wrong?" Marsha asked, obviously disappointed with my reaction. "They were brought about an hour ago, and they're as lovely as the ones last month. Aren't you going to look at the card?"

There was really no point in looking, but I put the mail on my desk and did, anyway. Inside the small envelope was a floral-bordered card with the words *I won't be forgetting* printed in block letters. I tossed it onto my desk and sat in the chair, and Marsha couldn't stand it.

"Ann, what's the *matter* with you?" she demanded, her huffiness laced with a definite motherly edge. "This is the second time in two months that someone has sent you a beautiful, expensive bouquet, and you won't say a word. You don't even look pleased."

"I'm not," I admitted. "I'm more annoyed, and this is the third time in three months. You were away helping your sister get over pneumonia when the first one came."

"That makes it even worse," she said, all but standing with fists on hips. "In three months you haven't said a single word about the man, not even a passing comment. You can't tell me he's another one who simply didn't work out, not when he refuses to give up. Ann, this one is different."

"I'll say," I agreed dryly, reaching for my coffee. "'Different' is definitely the word for him. I have my final report to dictate for the case file, so—"

"Absolutely not," Marsha interrupted, her brown eyes hard and her heavy arms folded. "I'm not moving an inch until you tell me all about him. I've spent the past two months guessing and waiting, but I'll die of old age before *you* get around to saying anything on your own. Unless, of course, you'd prefer that I mind my own business."

She looked straight at me when she said that, and I sighed before tasting my coffee. A good part of what Marsha did for me wasn't office business, which meant she didn't have to *keep* doing it. Her efforts simplified my life in a way I'd gotten used to, and if I refused to answer her questions...

"What would you like to know?" I asked, surrendering.

"You *know* what I want to know," she returned with fully justified satisfaction. "What's his name, what does he look like, where did you meet him—and what did he do that you aren't on the phone right now, thanking him for the flowers? He must have done *something*, but maybe it isn't as bad as you believe."

"You know, Marsha, I think I'm going to enjoy this after all," I told her with the beginnings of a grin. "If misery loves company, so does frustration. I have no idea what his name is or what he looks like, and we didn't exactly meet. That means I don't know who I would call even if I wanted to. Last month I tried tracing him through the florist, but it's a dead end.

The flowers were paid for in cash by a very young messenger, and the card was supplied by the shop. On top of that, a different florist was used each time. You now know exactly what I do about this very different man."

"But—that doesn't make any sense," she protested, sinking into the chair in front of my desk. "Are you saying he picked you out of thin air? If he hasn't introduced himself after three months, he must be one of those crazies. Have you called the police? If you haven't, then I'm going to."

"Marsha, no police," I said, and the warning note in my voice caught her attention. "I told you we never met, but our paths did cross once. Do you know what sort of business this firm handles?"

"Detective work," she answered promptly, then glanced over her shoulder. "I mean, confidential investigative work."

I nodded. "When you work in and around Washington, D.C., and deal with the problems of the monied, you sometimes find yourself tiptoeing around the edges of something official. I think there are more cloak-and-dagger groups working here than in any other capital in the world."

"So what else is new?" she commented. "Go on with the important part."

"That *is* the important part," I said, drinking a little more coffee. Then I told her the story, which she listened to carefully before sighing.

"So you know nothing about him, but he's been sending you flowers," she said, looking uncertain. "He knows who you are because you identified yourself to his friends, but you don't know who *he* is. What agency did they work for?"

"I don't know," I admitted. "If they'd wanted me to know, they would have told me."

"But if he doesn't intend to introduce himself, why does he keep sending flowers?" she asked with confusion. "Do you think there's something wrong with him—or that he's married?"

"Your guess is as good as mine, but I have an even better question," I countered. "How did he know I would be back in the office today? Last month's bouquet didn't come the very morning after I finished an assignment. Was he busy himself last month but is now back and checking up on me? His timing could be a coincidence, but somehow I don't believe it is. If he's following me, he has a hell of a lot of nerve."

To say the least. I tried to swallow my annoyance along with more coffee, but it didn't work. *I won't be forgetting*... What was *that* supposed to mean? I didn't want a guardian angel watching over me, as though I couldn't take care of myself. I wasn't the one who had been caught doing a simple undercover job.

And was that all he intended doing, just watching from a distance? If he was interested in more than simply being grateful, wouldn't he have already made a move? He could have arranged to meet me "accidentally" at almost any time, and that would have taken care of the requirements of secrecy.

But in three months' time, I hadn't even been approached by a bum looking for a handout. The dashing secret agent I'd saved was grateful enough to send flowers, but that was as far as it went. For any one of a hundred reasons, he would *not* be coming forward to introduce himself.

"If you ask me, it's a waste and a shame," Marsha pronounced, standing up. "He's probably the most beautiful man you can imagine, but he's too shy—or too married—to thank you properly. What's this world coming to, when even a woman's fantasies are ruined?"

I had to laugh at that, even though she wasn't far wrong. A mystery dream man *should* be exciting, but mine wasn't cutting it. Obviously I was doing something wrong, but before I could say that the intercom on my desk spoke up.

"Ann, would you step into my office, please?" Miller Houston's voice asked. "There are some people here I'd like you to meet."

"Coming, Miller," I responded, then got to my feet. "The bossman calls," I told Marsha. "Looks like it's going to be a while before I get around to that report. He was using the 'I've got a hot new assignment for you' tone of voice."

"He doesn't give you much time between assignments," Marsha observed. "How are you supposed to turn dreams into real life when you're forever running around working?"

"You think Miller wants me to lose the mystery man of my dreams?" I had to stop to laugh again. "Marsha, he's running a business I help to make very profitable, so of course he keeps me working. Wouldn't you?"

"No, not if it meant ruining your life," she answered, looking at me with serious brown eyes. "Why do you let him do it? Because you can't bring yourself to believe that dreams ever will become real?"

Observant woman, Marsha. I gave her a faint smile, then went to meet the people Miller Houston had in his office.

MILLER'S OFFICE was the largest in the suite, replete with three windows, thick carpeting, a giant desk and a lounge area for entertaining important potential clients. You could usually tell the net worth of his clients by where they were sitting—most were placed in the leather chairs in front of his desk.

The three people with him that morning were settled into the lounge area. They all had cups and saucers somewhere near them, and the large smoked-glass coffee table held a tray with a selection of cakes and rolls. Miller was clearly going all out for these people. When I closed the door he gestured me forward with a smile.

"Ann, thank you for coming so quickly," he said as he stood. "I'd like you to meet Mrs. Eleanor Tappan, her lovely daughter, Carrie, and her attorney, Mr. William Evans. Ladies and gentleman, Ann Mellion."

"Isn't she a bit too young to handle something of this importance?" Mrs. Tappan asked over the murmur of acknowledgment from her attorney.

She was an elegantly dressed woman who was probably in her fifties. Not that she looked it. Her light hair was perfectly arranged, her regal face was completely unlined, and her slender body was nicely rounded. Her expression said she was a shrewd, hard woman who didn't believe in compromise, and her light eyes indicated she wasn't easily pleased.

"One of Ann's greatest assets is the fact that she looks too young," Miller answered with a laugh. He'd naturally been expecting the objection, and was prepared to use it to his own advantage. "She's one of the best operatives I have, both discreet and capable, and

I think you can see how well she fits the current situation. Miss Tappan, would you stand?''

Carrie Tappan was in her late teens or early twenties. It wouldn't have been hard overlooking her, even if she'd been alone in the room. Her blond hair was a shade paler than her mother's, and so was her personality. Miller's speaking to her almost made her tremble. She stared at him with wide, embarrassed eyes.

''It's all right, darling,'' Mrs. Tappan said softly to the girl, patting one of her hands. ''Just stand up as Mr. Houston asked.''

The voice of authority might have been soft, but the girl had still been given an order she would not be allowed to disobey. Her reluctance was clear as she stood with the discomfort of someone who hated to be noticed. Miller certainly noticed her shyness but chose to ignore it.

''Thank you, Miss Tappan,'' he said with a smile. ''As I'm sure we can all see, Ann and Carrie are almost identical in build and coloring. Luck is with us on this one, and it would be a shame to throw it away. Ann is available right now, and can be ready to leave in twenty-four hours. Would you like a few moments alone to discuss the matter?''

''We would appreciate that, Mr. Houston,'' William Evans answered with a weary smile. His age must have been close to Mrs. Tappan's, but on him it didn't come off nearly as well. He had the long-suffering look of someone whose business demanded he cater to people he didn't like, but he also appeared competent. His client inclined her head in agreement.

''Then please stay where you are,'' Miller told them with another smile. ''Ann and I will wait in my anteroom until you're ready. Just knock on the door, and we'll be right back with you."

He got his coffee cup from the table before leading the way to the small sitting room just off his office. The room was used for a lot of things, including private talks with those selling information. Another door led to a back way out of the offices. Miller closed the door we'd come through, then sat in one of the chairs.

"It shouldn't take them very long to decide to go ahead with it," he told me. "You *are* all through with your last assignment?"

"It wasn't any of the maids doing the pilfering," I answered with a nod. "The youngest daughter had a friend with a habit to support, and stealing from others was a better idea than taking from her own home. They were all in shock when I broke the news. Kids from wealthy families are supposed to be immune to the common problems of the world."

"I'd like to think I'd be smarter in their place," he said with a shake of his head. "Chances are I'd be just as blind. But this one should be easier for you. Rather than being a maid, you'll be Miss Carrie Tappan herself."

"Mrs. Tappan wants it, so the lawyer won't be able to talk her out of it," I observed, sipping at what was left of my coffee. "He must be the one who brought her here, so why is he against the idea of hiring us?"

"He thinks it's a waste of money," Miller replied with a shrug, dismissing the idea. "Mr. and Mrs. Tappan are having a difference of opinion, and the lady finds it impolitic to refuse her husband's wishes right now. Mr. Tappan is in the foreign service and is in line for a promotion. He'll be given his choice of posts, and the lady wants to be sure he chooses the one *she* prefers."

"You didn't get all that from them," I stated, studying his smooth, bland face. Miller Houston attended official parties and receptions on a regular basis, and no one ever noticed how hard he was listening. If it was happening in D.C. and someone besides the principals knew about it, chances were that someone was Miller.

"Having the latest gossip helps me run this place more efficiently," he said with a grin. "That's how I know the lady will choose to hire us. Young Miss Tappan has been named as a beneficiary in her father's brother-in-law's will, but she has to show up at the reading in Louisiana. Her father, a believer in strong family ties, wants her to go. Her mother, who never approved of that branch of her husband's family, doesn't. That part I did get from Mrs. Tappan."

"I'll give you odds that dear Mrs. Tappan isn't free to leave the city for a while," I offered. "If she were, she'd be taking her darling to Louisiana herself. Since she can't go, baby won't be allowed to go alone. The child might get the idea she can get along by herself if she's let off the leash."

"We're not here to tell people they're ruining their children," he said. "If Mrs. Tappan wants to hire a stand-in for her daughter, it's up to us to provide that stand-in. With her husband out of the country for a while, she can respect his wishes without actually turning the girl loose. Are you going to have a problem with that?"

"Not really," I said, looking away from him. "I'm sorry—every once in a while I find myself up on a soapbox without remembering how I got there. Anyway, if I'm going to double for the girl, I'll need some time with her to pick up the essentials."

"You won't need all that much," Miller disagreed. "The only time the girl came in contact with her uncle was at her christening. Her father invited his sister and brother-in-law to be the girl's godparents, and they were. Shortly after that they returned to the family home in Louisiana, and there was no visiting back and forth."

"So I go down for the reading of the will, thank everyone politely, then come back," I summed up with a nod. "It sounds like the vacation I've been wanting to take."

"Once you get back we'll talk about a vacation," he said, his smile the same one he always showed when I mentioned taking time off from work. "If there's nothing high priority waiting for your special touch, I'm sure we'll work something out. And you won't be going to Louisiana alone."

"Isn't it carrying things a little too far to refuse to let your daughter's *stand-in* off the leash?" I asked with brows raised. "I've heard of possessive, but that's too much."

"Come down off that soapbox, Tommy," he said, chuckling. "Mr. Evans is the one who insists on sending someone from his office with you. You and your companion will have power of attorney from Miss Tappan, to make your use of her name legal. Just in case the bequest turns out to be substantial, Mr. Evans wants to be sure it isn't lost to the girl through mishandling."

"He's probably more interested in making sure I don't commit the girl to something Mommy would disapprove of," I said with a grimace. "And I'd appreciate it if you would stop calling me 'Tommy.' The others do it because you do, and I'm tired of it."

"When you stop being a tomboy, I'll stop calling you 'Tommy,'" he countered, very amused. "You may occasionally dress like a proper young lady, but proper young ladies don't leap to the top of soapboxes in a single bound."

"You may not have noticed, Miller, but I don't take well to blackmail." If my amusement wasn't as great as his, it wasn't off by much. "You have until I get back to reconsider your position. If you haven't thought better of the decision, then I get tough. And believe me, you won't like me when I'm tough."

"*Tsk, tsk,* threatening your boss," he said as he watched me stand.

"I'll be in my office working on a report," I said, very aware of the glint in his dark eyes. "Let me know when the clients make their decision."

"And ignoring people is very bad manners," he called after me softly as I took the back way out. "Don't you ever want to grow up enough to take over my job?"

I didn't quite stop in mid-stride, but that doesn't mean I wasn't shocked. Was that what Miller had in mind for me? I went back to my office, but instead of doing the report, I thought about what he'd said.

Miller had given up having a family to make the agency what it was. Did I want to do the same? If he was serious, did I want the chance to try? Would it be that much of a sacrifice to give up something I didn't even have? The questions flew round and round in my mind, and it was a relief when I was called back to Miller's office.

On my way out, I didn't even glance at the beautiful flowers sitting on my desk.

Chapter Two

It was two days before I was able to leave, but that didn't throw me off schedule. Mrs. Tappan had planned for the possibility of not finding an immediate stand-in for her daughter and had allowed for a delay. It was nice to have the extra time, and I made good use of it.

It took only a little while to get Carrie's life story from her mother. Mrs. Tappan didn't bother to stand when a maid showed me into the living room, but instead gestured to a chair.

"Do sit down, Ms. Mellion," she invited coolly. "I understand you need the details of my daughter's life."

"That's right," I agreed, sitting in the indicated place. "As much as you can tell me, including likes and dislikes. I'll be taking notes."

I pulled out a notebook and pen to prove the point, then looked at her as I waited. A cup of coffee would have gone well right about then, and I wondered why she hadn't offered any. Then I suddenly realized why: although she had one of her own, those of her imagined class didn't offer refreshments to employees.

"My Carrie is perfect," Mrs. Tappan said when she was certain she had my full attention. "As a very small child she was a trifle high-spirited, but she soon outgrew that. She became polite and obedient and never disobeyed her father or me. We're quite proud of her."

"I'm sure," I murmured, fighting not to comment. "What I need, though, Mrs. Tappan, is facts. Where she went to school, what awards she won, who her friends are, what talents she's shown. Any trait that someone might find out by researching her and will notice if I don't also know it or exhibit it. Habits, taste in reading, hobbies, things like that."

"You act as if you expect this impersonation to go on for months," she said with a cultured frown. "Since it will only be for a matter of days, I don't know why you're being so—inquisitive. If someone asks you questions about Carrie, just ignore them or refuse to answer."

"You've just made my point for me," I said. "I'm going to be traveling as Carrie Tappan, and after no more than a five-minute acquaintance with her I already know she'd never do as you just suggested. It would be totally out of character for her to refuse to tell anyone anything, and it isn't always possible to ignore people. If you want this done right, you have to tell me what I need to know. If you don't care to cooperate, find a firm that doesn't care whether it succeeds. Chandler and Rich has a reputation to maintain, and we don't do that by being sloppy."

I finished my speech and sat back to wait for her decision. I'd decided a more forceful attitude was necessary with someone like Mrs. Tappan, who was too used to dealing with underlings. If you pay the bills you're entitled to call the shots, but there's a limit.

"Perhaps you should have been told that I dislike high-handedness," she said after a moment, reaching for the coffee cup that stood on a small table near her. "Your employer, Mr. Houston, is well aware of that, but apparently you aren't. Shall I call him to discuss the shortcomings of his staff?"

"You can call him to discuss anything you like," I said, closing my pen and starting to put it and the notebook away. "Miller would never expect me to go into an assignment unprepared, not even for the kind of fee he's charging you. Our reputation is worth more than twenty such fees, and if we lose it we'll never get it back."

"Just a moment," she said, finally believing that I really was leaving. "Are you saying your job means so little to you that you'd jeopardize it in the hope that Mr. Houston will agree with you? If he doesn't, which might very well be the case, you'll find yourself suddenly unemployed."

I sighed. "Mrs. Tappan, this isn't a job for me—it's a career. I'm good at what I do and our competition knows it, which means unemployment doesn't frighten me. If you want this job done properly, you'll leave it to us to decide what is or isn't necessary. If you want it done your way alone, you really will have to look elsewhere. I'm sure there's a firm somewhere that doesn't mind sending its people in blind."

The woman had a passion for running things, one that amounted to compulsion. This time she'd have to swallow the compulsion or find another firm to do her dirty work. I'll admit I didn't like her, but that had little to do with my attitude. I'm enough of a professional to do my job properly no matter who is involved, and if Miller had been there he would have been on my side.

"William Evans tells me that Chandler and Rich is the best to be had," she said at last, after taking another sip of coffee. "Since I don't believe in making do with second best, I'll obviously have to put up with your...creative tantrums, just as I did with the man who decorated this house for me. What was it you said you needed to know?"

I repeated the list while I got the pen and pad ready again, keeping my face expressionless as I reminded myself that I was a professional. If she wanted to pretend that she was indulging my "creative tantrums" rather than admit she'd lost the argument, that was her business. As long as I got what I needed I shouldn't care, and I didn't. It was just so damned annoying....

"Carrie went to a private school, of course," Mrs. Tappan began. "Hogarth Academy, but you've probably never heard of it. They certainly don't advertise and are very careful about the children they accept. Only from the best families, a rule they refuse to break. Carrie's grades were adequate in unnecessary subjects, much higher with the things that count. Hogarth Academy valued her as a student."

I dutifully made notes, privately interpreting what I'd been told. Carrie had gone to a school that enjoyed getting her father's money, and they'd floated her through as discreetly as possible. She hadn't covered herself with academic glory, but they'd given her enough meaningless fill-in subjects that even a corpse could have passed them. Because of that she'd been able to graduate, which had more than satisfied her parents.

"What about friends?" I prompted. "Was there anyone she became close with, anyone she kept in contact with? I need to know if I'm likely to run into anyone who could recognize her, even from a few years ago."

"My daughter is very careful about relationships, even when the girls come from acceptable backgrounds" I was told with a cool smile. "She was acquainted with everyone at Hogarth, of course, but considered it unnecessary to keep in touch after graduation. These days she occasionally sees the daughters of *my* friends and acquaintances, but still prefers to hold herself aloof."

Too repressed to make friends at school, I wrote in my version of shorthand. Now forced to associate only with those her mother approves of. Probably wouldn't know what to do with a friend even if she had one. Forget about asking again about awards and talents. If there had been any, Mommy would have mentioned them first thing.

"Does she do a lot of reading?" I asked without looking up. "What about things she does all the time, like bicycling at three in the afternoon every day? How about hobbies, things she enjoys doing whenever she has the time?"

"My daughter reads the classics when she wants to read," was the self-satisfied answer. "She has no interest in the trash they print these days, which shows her excellent taste. The only things she makes a habit of doing are proper things, like working on my charity committees four times a year and attending certain society functions. With a schedule like that, she has no time for hobbies, and wouldn't indulge in them in any event. She learned better at finishing school."

"Finishing school," I echoed, wondering how the girl kept from going crazy. "I didn't realize they still had that sort of thing. These days, those who can afford it usually go on to college."

"A waste of time as well as money," Mrs. Tappan stated, her disapproval clear. "A girl in Carrie's position has no need to be bored with useless, unnecessary learning. When she marries her husband will provide for her, and her duty will be to provide an attractive home and be a proper hostess. Those are the essentials of her life, and she learned them at finishing school. Colleges these days are filled with nothing but riffraff, an outrage there was no need to subject her to."

"Outrage" was the proper word, but I just sat there taking notes. Everything was being voiced as Carrie's ideas and preferences, yet there wasn't a chance they really were. A girl who thought that way would be arrogant and selfishly indulgent, not shy to the point of invisibility. It wasn't hard, however, to figure out who the opinions did belong to.

"What about trips she's taken and places she's seen?" I asked, trying to get some hint of the girl herself. "Has she ever vacationed somewhere with a—an acquaintance, or alone?"

"I've taken her to London, Paris and Rome, of course," Mrs. Tappan answered with a negligent wave of her hand. "Actually, we visit England two or three times a year, and if Ambassador Tappan accepts a post there, we'll relocate. But she certainly does *not* travel alone, nor in the company of someone who isn't close to her. My daughter is a lady, Ms. Mellion, not a tramp."

I really wanted to point out that that sentiment would be great for a movie, possibly about a couple of cartoon dogs. As a test in self-control, keeping quiet was a doozy. Somehow I made it, though, and then was saved by the appearance of the maid.

"Mrs. Tappan, you asked me to remind you," the woman said diffidently. "You should be leaving right now for your luncheon."

"Thank you, Mary," my hostess said, pushing away her cup before standing. "I'm sure you understand, Ms. Mellion. My time isn't my own. I do hope you have everything you need."

"Everything but a look at your daughter's wardrobe," I answered casually, also preparing to get up. "Since I'll be leaving tomorrow, I'll need the rest of today to buy clothes of my own to match."

By then I was standing and looking straight at her, which meant that I saw the vexation flash in her eyes. She'd planned to get rid of me on her own schedule all along, whether or not we were through. The only problem was, I now had a requirement she couldn't dismiss. I was certain she did have a luncheon to attend and was caught in a dilemma. Being the helpful, thoughtful soul that I am, though, I was all prepared to help her out.

"But you certainly don't need to delay your departure just to give me a fifteen-minute tour of someone's closet," I added smoothly. "Your maid will be fine for that."

"Yes, I suppose that's so," she said grudgingly, then hardened to the reality when she found no alternative. "Well, I can't be late, so there's really no choice. I'll arrange it when Mary comes back with my coat."

I nodded to acknowledge the decision, smiling only on the inside. If I'd said I wanted to talk to Carrie herself, she would have had me thrown out on the spot. She took a compact and lipstick from her purse to freshen her makeup, then the maid returned. Mary held the white cashmere coat for her employer, and once the belt was tied Mrs. Tappan turned to her.

"Mary, Ms. Mellion needs to see Miss Carrie's clothes." She stopped abruptly, apparently realizing that she didn't have a reason *why* I needed to. If she didn't explain it, the woman might begin wondering.

"For the article I'm doing on the ambassador's family," I supplied with a reporterlike smile. "The ladies who read our magazine want to know simply everything, and you certainly can't blame them. Thank you again for your time, Mrs. Tappan, and I'll be sure to mention that impressive luncheon in my article."

"Yes, of course," my hostess said, then headed for the door. "Just see to it, Mary. I'm already late."

She exited to the words of "Yes, Mrs. Tappan," then the door was closed behind her. As the maid came back toward me I heard a car—chauffeured, no doubt—accelerate down the drive, and that was all I needed. I waited until the woman reached me, then gave her another smile.

"I wonder if you would find Miss Tappan for me," I said. "I'd rather not paw through someone's things without their being there. You understand, don't you?"

"Yes, it so happens I do," the woman answered with a smile of her own. "Wait here a moment, please."

With Eleanor Tappan gone, the big house seemed empty. Carrie appeared after a couple of minutes to lead me upstairs. Her discomfort was obvious from the way she drew back inside herself, and she gestured me after her rather than speaking.

"Don't worry, Miss Tappan, this won't take long," I said, but the reassurance made no impression. She moved quietly ahead of me up the stairs and along the hall, and from there into a beautifully furnished bedroom. As a matter of fact, the room was downright elegant, like a display in an exclusive furniture store.

"It's too bad you couldn't decorate this room the way *you* wanted to," I said, the comment slipping out before I could stop it. "I mean, it's really lovely, so nicely—"

"How did you know?" she asked, cutting off my attempt to backtrack. "This *isn't* what I'd wanted in here, but how did you know?"

The words were softly spoken, but I felt a strange intensity behind them. Carrie's light eyes were looking directly at me, her withdrawal having vanished.

"The room isn't lived in," I answered. "It lacks the personal touches of a place someone considers their own. But I shouldn't have said what I did, and I apologize. I *am* supposed to observe things, but not blurt them out."

"People do that all the time around me," she said, and where someone else might have smiled faintly, she didn't. "It's as though they consider themselves all alone. Did you know I wanted to go on this trip?"

"No, I didn't," I responded.

"Being at school was boring and confining, but at least I wasn't *here,*" she went on, looking slowly around. "I've spent my whole life in this room, but it still refuses to accept me. I thought if I met strangers, people who don't know me..."

"Then why not do it?" I couldn't help asking when her words trailed off. Miller would kill me, but there was such wistful longing in her voice. "You can tell your mother you'd rather not have someone pretending to be you. She does know how you feel, doesn't she?"

"No, she doesn't," Carried answered, then walked toward the sliding doors in one wall. "My closet is here."

I followed after, and once again felt I was following an empty space. Carrie had withdrawn again, fading back into the woodwork.

The clothes in the wardrobe reflected their owner. Bland winter grays and tans, summer pastels, none of it colored to make a head turn even once. Every bit of it was expensive and classically beautiful, but it suited the room more than the occupant. Since it was exactly what I'd been expecting, the inspection tour was over in about a minute and a half.

"Well, that does it," I said as I turned away from the neat, perfectly arranged racks. "Thank you for your time and for allowing the invasion, Miss Tappan. When I get back and make my report, you'll probably be glad you didn't go. It won't be anything but a dull trip, dull people and dull happenings."

"My mother doesn't know how I feel because I didn't tell her," Carrie whispered. She was back to our previous conversation, and her eyes were full of pain. "My mother doesn't want me to go, and I've never been able to win against her. I never will win, so what does it matter?"

"Never have doesn't mean never will," I countered. She was talking to me like that, I thought, because she so desperately needed *someone* to talk to.

"And there's something else you need to understand," I added, deliberately not being kind. "Other people, no matter how strong, are stronger than you only when you let them be. If you say no to something and then let yourself be talked around, or if you don't even say no to begin with, that's your doing, not someone else's."

By that time she was staring at me with an expression I couldn't interpret. It had pain and shock and confusion and who knows what else, and then she hurried from the room. She didn't run, of course, since proper young ladies don't run, but she definitely moved faster than usual. I silently cursed my big mouth before going after her, but when I reached the hall she was gone. Like a ghost, I felt, the living ghost she seemed destined to be for the rest of her life.

But at least I'd gotten a better feel for her personality, which was what I'd needed. I found my own way out of the Tappan house, and after a quick lunch I went shopping. The clothes I bought would all go on the expense account, and after the Tappans paid for them I'd probably get rid of them. Or maybe give them to Carrie. She and I were just about the same size, and every bit of it was bland enough to delight her mother. I thought about getting luggage, as well, then decided against it. Mine was cream colored, and Carrie would have traveled often enough with her parents that hers would not be brand-new.

It wasn't very late when I got home with my purchases, but it was late enough that no messages on my machine meant something. If Carrie had told her mother about our conversation, Miller would certainly have called by now to say the trip was off. After thinking about it all afternoon, I almost wished Carrie *had* told her mother. It would probably have been the first uncontrolled action of her life, and might have done some good.

I MADE DINNER, packed for the next day's trip, then soaked in a hot bath while reviewing my notes. The details of Carrie Tappan's life weren't hard to remember, and they made me certain about one thing at least: no one would be popping up to say they knew the real Carrie and I wasn't her. It was highly unlikely that anyone knew the real Carrie, and even if they'd met her, they weren't likely to remember.

I was able to get to bed early that night—one questionable benefit in living alone—and it turned out to be a good thing. Bright and early the next morning my phone rang, and it was Miller Houston.

"Tommy, there's a small change in plans you need to know about," he said. "A messenger is on his way to your place with that limited power of attorney, and after you sign it he'll witness your signature and then take it back. It's going to be the only power of attorney."

"What about the one my traveling companion is supposed to have?" I asked, finally forgetting about the possibility of Carrie telling on me. If she hadn't done it by then, she never would. "I thought that lawyer Evans wanted everyone involved to be covered."

"He did, but it must have occurred to someone that secrets shared are secrets told. Mrs. Tappan doesn't want her husband to find out about this, so they've limited the number of people who know. The law clerk going with you, James Nolan, has been told he'll be traveling with Miss Carrie Tappan to keep an unofficial eye on her interests. Ann Mellion is someone he's never heard of and won't ever meet."

"So it starts at the airport, and doesn't end until I get back," I said with resignation. "It would have been nice to have someone there to relax with, but this way I don't have to worry about slips. No one will know, so I have to make sure it stays like that. No loose lips, no sunken ships."

Miller chuckled. "That also applies to the messenger. He doesn't know what he's carrying, so sign it without discussion, then seal it away. And when you've got this wrapped up, call me from the airport in New Orleans. If the timing works right, I just may have a really important one for you."

"What about that vacation we were supposed to talk about?" I couldn't keep from reminding him. "It's almost two years since the last time I got away, and you called me back for an emergency almost before I unpacked."

"Tommy, do I have to tell you timing is everything?" he asked in that gently lecturing way he had. "Vacations can be taken any time, but important cases have to be grabbed when they show up. Think about your career and then tell me how a vacation will advance it."

He actually waited for me to tell him what he knew he'd never hear, but I suppose my silence was what he was really after. I know there are men in this world who disapprove of the idea of a woman having a career; every once in a while I wished Miller were one of them.

"So we'll see how the timing goes, and take it from there," he said, ending the disagreement. "Don't forget you said this assignment would be like a vacation, so take advantage of it and enjoy yourself. We'll talk again when it's over."

"Right," I muttered as I hung up. Enjoy myself playing a ghost. And think about my career instead of choosing between vacation spots. On vacation I would have had the chance to relax, meet interesting men, but while advancing my career... Well, thinking about that would have to wait for another time.

I was dressed by the time the messenger arrived. He handed me a large, sealed envelope with William Evans's signature scrawled across the flap. Inside was a new envelope, a cover letter, and the power-of-attorney agreement, which I scanned before signing. The messenger witnessed my signature and notarized it, then waited while I folded the agreement and the old envelope and sealed them both in the new envelope. Signing on the flap fulfilled the last of the instructions in the cover letter, and that was that.

Dulles International Airport was the same madhouse it usually was, but at least I didn't have to wait in the longest line. With the reservation made, I just had to pick up my ticket and boarding pass, then could hand over my luggage and head for the proper gate. Since I had started being Carrie Tappan the minute I left my apartment, no one so much as glanced at me twice.

When I reached the proper gate for my flight, I was still almost an hour early. It felt strange not to be rushing through, racing to make a last-minute flight that was being held for me. That was the way I usually used airports, on the fly while on the job. Even the last time I'd gone on vacation—

"Excuse me," a baritone voice interrupted. "Are you Miss Tappan? I'm James Nolan."

I looked up at the man who had spoken, and it was difficult not to respond to his smile. In his early thirties, dark-haired and blue-eyed, James Nolan was impressive in a broad-shouldered way. If his gray suit wasn't a Marmons it was a very good copy, and his silk tie represented one of the Ivy League schools. He was also one of the handsomest men I'd ever seen, and nothing like what I'd been expecting.

"Have I made a mistake?" he asked, that beautiful smile faltering. "Aren't you Miss Carrie Tappan?"

"Yes, I am," I answered in the quietly withdrawn way Carrie would have. "How did you know?"

"I was told to look for the prettiest blonde in the airport," he responded with a grin, obviously teasing. "Not to mention the fact that you seem to be the only young blond female on our flight. Would you like to have a drink while we're waiting to board?"

"A drink," I echoed. "I'm not sure there's enough time..."

"If we make it coffee there's plenty of time," he assured me with another of those smiles. "The snack bar's right over there, so let's not keep it waiting."

He was gentle in the way he urged me along with him, but he was also firm. The hand in the middle of my back said he wasn't about to take no for an answer, no matter how shy I was. William Evans had obviously told him a thing or two about Carrie Tappan, which may not have been a good idea. If I accidentally did something out of character, James Nolan might be in a position to notice.

"You sit right here and save this table for us, and I'll get the coffee," my companion said, pulling out a chair. "How do you take yours?"

"Black, please," I answered in a small voice as I sat. I wasn't looking at him, and hadn't been for the past few minutes.

"Black it is," he agreed pleasantly, then headed for the trays. At that point I was able to watch him, and confirmed the fact that he carried no briefcase. They didn't want him to look official, then.

But the way he did look was a problem. I'd felt his attraction right from the start, but how would the real Carrie Tappan react? Would she be frightened by a man that handsome? Horribly, uncontrollably attracted? Uninterested because he didn't have her mother's explicit approval? I'd intended to ignore James Nolan, but I'd pictured him as quiet and studious or professionally withdrawn. The James Nolan I'd just met wasn't going to *let* himself be ignored.

That made for an immediate problem. I watched the man at the coffee dispenser, noticing that the girl behind the counter was also watching him. It would have been nice getting to know him, possibly laying a foundation for the future, but that was out. Carrie Tappan and James Nolan couldn't meet—even by chance—when they got back to town, and Ann Mellion was a name he was never supposed to learn.

"Thanks, Miller," I muttered with a sigh. I would have to associate with the man but couldn't give him any encouragement at all.

James Nolan stood on line to pay for the coffees, then brought the tray to the table. The snack bar was full, but there weren't so many people that someone had tried to share our company. He put a cup in front of me, one in his place, then sat down to my right.

"Now, then," he said, and the smile was back. "Since we'll be spending the next few days together, I'm Jim and you're Carrie. You're probably wondering why I'm just a law clerk at my age, Carrie, so I'll tell you. I hadn't wanted to join the family firm so I resisted, but the lure of the law finally got me. Once I pass the bar I may go back to my father and brothers, but then, I may not. I'll decide when the time comes. Now I'd like to hear about you."

"I'm sure Mr. Evans said it all," I murmured, toying with my coffee cup. "There's no sense in repeating what you already know."

"All Bill told me was that you were extremely quiet," Nolan responded evenly. "He also said I wasn't to make you do anything you didn't want to. Does that mean I'm not even allowed to try to make you change your mind?"

I looked up to see the faint smile on his face, emphasized by the way he'd folded his arms on the table in front of his cup. I'd met confident men with less charm than James Nolan; it was a shame it had to go to waste.

"That's silly, Mr. Nolan," I said with a direct look. "Why would you want to make me change my mind? And what would I be changing it about?"

"Why, about not doing something I wanted us to do together," he answered, almost flustered. "You're a very pretty girl, Carrie, something I'm sure I'm not the first to notice. Since we'll be together for the next few days, I'd like to get to know you."

"Oh, that's even sillier," I said with a faint smile. "I'm not pretty, Mr. Nolan, and I know it. You're saying that just to be nice, but there's no need."

"But, Carrie, I'm serious," he protested. "I think you're very pretty, and I do want to get to know you."

I let my smile widen as I shook my head and looked away, but not before I saw the flash of frustration in his blue eyes. My flatly refusing to believe his interest would either drive him crazy or turn him off, but either way it would keep things from developing. Carrie Tappan thought she wasn't pretty, and nothing would get her to change her mind.

We were just about finished with our coffee when the first boarding call came, and the two of us walked silently to the gate. He'd apparently decided to slow his advances to put me at ease, but he certainly hadn't given up. His attitude was friendly but determined, and mine was shyly disbelieving. It would be interesting to see how long his determination lasted.

I had the window seat for the flight, but couldn't enjoy the takeoff as much as I usually do. Showing a preference for *anything* would have given my traveling companion a chance to share it, and that was the first step toward building a relationship.

What we did share was more coffee; as we drank it we decided what to tell people about James Nolan. His suggestion was that he be introduced as my financial adviser, someone who would let me know what to do with my inheritance. If the bequest was small it would make no difference, but large inheritances have financial consequences. Bringing a lawyer would be a tacky way of saying I didn't trust the people I would soon meet, but a financial adviser should be perfectly acceptable.

I quietly agreed but privately wondered about the real reason for his being there. Originally he was supposed to have known that I wasn't Carrie Tappan. Had William Evans sent him to make sure I did nothing to sully the Tappan name? At that point there was no way of knowing, but I'd certainly find out.

Landing in New Orleans was uneventful, and we headed downstairs to claim our luggage. The carousel area was being renovated, and giant canvases hung in front of wall sections, metal frameworks stood unattended, and whole stretches of unfinished sections were unlit. Because of that the place looked like an enormous cave, dim under the inadequate lighting that *was* being used.

"There must be a dozen or more conventions being held in the city," James Nolan said as he looked around. "I can't ever remember seeing crowds like this when it wasn't a holiday. There's no sense in both of us fighting our way through them, so you stay here while I claim our luggage. After that we can try to find the car that was supposed to meet us, assuming they've gotten here. We landed early."

Arguing would have been out of character, so I told him the color of my luggage and surrendered my claim checks. He turned away and two steps later he was gone from sight, swallowed by the crowds he'd mentioned.

I brushed at the skirt of my pearl-blue silk dress, watching the way everyone passed me without a second glance. I stood not far from the limousine counter; if our ride didn't show up, we'd probably have to use a limousine. There was lots of humidity in the air, which was beginning to make me sweat, and I wished we were already on our way. The sooner we got there the sooner it would be over.

"Excuse me, Miss, but your car is ready," a voice said from my right. I looked around to see a uniformed chauffeur, and he gave me an oddly forced smile. "If you'll follow me, we'll get you settled and comfy in no time."

"Comfy?" I almost echoed, but quickly thought better of it. Instead I gave him a ghost of a smile and said, "My traveling companion is getting the luggage. If you help him—"

"Oh, I'm sure he can take care of it," the man interrupted in a too-jovial way. "Or, if you want, I'll come back after you're in the car. A lady like you shouldn't be standing here all alone."

"I don't mind," I said, beginning to get the strangest feeling. "If I get separated from my companion in this madhouse, I may never find him again. But if you like I can go with you to where he is, then—"

"Let's talk about it in the car," the man interrupted again, this time without the smile. "It's right this way."

His right hand came to my left arm as though he were helping me, but the fingers of that big hand closed tight. I wasn't being helped, I was being forced, and he didn't care that he was hurting me.

Unbelievably, it looked like I was being kidnapped!

Chapter Three

Normally, it isn't hard to free yourself in a situation like that when you know what you're doing, but I had an additional problem. Carrie Tappan wasn't supposed to know how to take care of herself, and that's who I had to continue to be.

The uniformed stranger was trying to force me toward one of the exits and attempting not to be obvious about it. Carrie Tappan wasn't likely to scream and make a scene, so the man wasn't wrong to believe he could simply walk me out. I wasn't the sort to scream, either, not when I had so many other choices.

Tripping the man who held my arm just took the proper timing, and as we both stumbled I managed to wrench myself free. The move I used to break his hold is simple enough to look like an accidental jerk, but I also made sure to stumble into the man while he was off balance. He had to use both hands to keep himself from going face first into the concrete floor, which allowed me to slip away into the crowd before he could grab for me again.

Behind me I heard the exclamations of concerned people as I hurried away. Not knowing whether he would follow me, I had to keep myself from pushing people out of my way. If he did decide to come after me again...

"Carrie, where did you disappear to?" James Nolan demanded, suddenly right there in front of me. "They still haven't unloaded the luggage, so I came back to— Are you all right? What's happened?"

His hands came to my arms as he took a really good look at me, then one of those arms was around me while he led the way out of the crowds. When we reached the spot I'd originally been standing on I scanned the nearest faces, but the man in chauffeur's uniform wasn't among them.

"Now tell me what happened," Nolan ordered, using one hand to brush back some of my hair. "You look like you've been running through the airport, and that doesn't make any sense."

"A man—tried—to kidnap me," I whispered, groping for the proper words. "He had my arm and refused to let go, but when he tripped I got away from him. I was so afraid..."

"Well, of course you were!" he answered with shock, then anger took over and his arm tightened. "If I get my hands on him, I'll— What did he look like, Carrie?"

"He was wearing a chauffeur's uniform," I said, still being cautious. "His face was very average, and he also wore a cap. Shouldn't we call the police?"

"That's an excellent idea," he said, smoothing my hair again. "But first I want to know more about what happened. The man just said your name and took your arm, then began dragging you off? I must have been too far away to hear you scream."

"I—I didn't scream," I admitted, almost feeling as if the police were already grilling me. "And he didn't call me by name. He just said the car was waiting. I wanted to find you first, but he refused to listen. He took my arm and forced me to go along with him."

"I think we'd better forget about calling the police," Nolan said after taking a deep breath.

"But why?" I asked, struggling to remember to keep my voice soft. "If we call them right away they might catch him and then—"

"And then they'd be able to let him go again," Nolan interrupted with patience in his tone as he looked down at me. "You said he didn't use your name. What if he was here to pick up someone else and came to you by mistake? If he works for the girl's father and was told the girl would be stubborn about coming home... You see how innocent it all could have been?"

"But he refused to go and find *you,*" I pointed out. "If it was all that innocent, why would he have refused?"

"If he was after another girl, it had to be her unacceptable boyfriend he refused to go looking for," Nolan countered. "And now that I think about it, that sounds like the most reasonable explanation. After all, why on earth would anyone want to kidnap you? You don't have a secret life in crime, do you?"

His grin brought some warmth to my cheeks, but his point was well taken. There was no reason for anyone to kidnap Carrie Tappan, so it must have been the mistake Nolan suggested. I felt a little foolish for not having thought of the explanation myself.

"Let's just forget about it," I decided. "It was a case of mistaken identity, but when you go back for the luggage I'm going with you."

"You'd better believe you are," he agreed with another grin. "If I let an attractive woman avoid my company by claiming to be kidnapped, it could set a precedent. Let's go back right now."

He took my arm without noticing my sigh, and we went looking for the carousel with our bags. The incident hadn't helped my plan to keep Nolan at a discouraging distance, and now I would have to work harder to make it happen. I admire persistence in a man, but there are certain times...

Most of the luggage was gone when we reached the carousel, so we claimed ours quickly, found a skycap with a hand truck, and went back to the limo counter. By then there was a young man in a shiny blue suit holding up a sign with the name Tappan on it.

"This is Miss Tappan," Nolan told the young man with a smile, gesturing to me. "And your timing is excellent. We were just about to hire a car."

"When I saw your plane was already in, I knew I'd probably find you here," the man said with no friendliness whatsoever. "I'm Daniel, and the car is this way."

After his hearty welcome, Daniel led us to where he'd parked a stately old limousine. He reluctantly helped the skycap unload the luggage into the trunk after he'd just as reluctantly handed us into the car, and five minutes later we were on our way. It was clear that our driver knew his way around despite being rather young and sour.

Daniel ignored the green exit signs on the highway for the longest time. Then, after passing a large plastic cow, he suddenly turned onto a well-worn but almost empty road. That was the one we stayed on for quite a while, with only an occasional house on either side. But there were certainly a lot of trees, and their shade made the cloudy day even dimmer. In the presence of sunshine, the area would have been really beautiful.

"Looks like we're almost there," Nolan commented when we turned onto what was obviously a private road. He'd been silently watching the scenery until then, the way I had.

"Only another mile or so," Daniel answered, sounding as if our simply talking was an imposition. Then he added, "Don't let the look of the house make you start yelling at me to take you back to the city. Mrs. Allyn never let it be prettied up on the outside, but inside everything is modern. Even if you can't always see it."

Nolan and I exchanged glances over that mysterious statement, but it seemed smarter to wait before asking any questions. Once the house came into view, we understood part of what we'd been told. A large, old Southern mansion appeared, and the closer we got the older it looked. White paint can only do so much, and the humidity of the region hadn't been kind to the house. *Rambling* was the word that first came to mind, right along with *Gothic*. Sunshine would have made it look shabby, but clouds clearly turned it brooding.

"You said everything inside is modern," Nolan remarked after studying the place. "Does that mean the doors to the secret passages work on electric eyes, or that the ghosts show up in jeans and T-shirts? And how well do you know the butler?"

"That's really clever, but I guess you could say *I'm* the butler," Daniel answered, now sounding indignant as well as displeased. "My mother is the housekeeper, but since the house will probably be closed after the will is read, she's using only a skeleton staff.

I got volunteered to help after the other heirs arrived, and I don't like it. I'm on vacation from school in Texas, and you can bet I'm not studying to be a servant."

I could sympathize with his problem even if I didn't appreciate his attitude, but I forgot both as we pulled up in front of the house. The drive was gravel, of course, but the sound of our arrival failed to bring anyone to the front door.

"I'll take you inside, then come back for your bags," Daniel said before getting out to circle the car. He opened the door on my side, actually helped me across the gravel to the steps, then went back to close the car door behind Nolan. It didn't take him long to come back again, but the humidity was already doing a good job of making us wilt.

Daniel opened one of the front doors, and we followed him inside to discover one of the modern conveniences he'd mentioned. The wide entrance hall was air-conditioned, and walking into it was like crossing into another world.

"Wait here and I'll get my mother," Daniel said after quickly closing out the heat. "She's probably back in the kitchen, checking on dinner."

He took off through a door to my right. Most of my attention was on the entrance hall, which was imposing in a lavish, Hollywood way. A wide and regal staircase rose directly opposite the front doors, traveling all the way up to the second floor. The strip of hallway showing at the top of the stairs had a wrought-iron railing in front of it, and the carpeting on the stairs seemed to continue along the hallway.

"Those lamps on the walls aren't gas lamps," Nolan said with a hint of quiet satisfaction. "They're not very bright, but they're definitely electric. I wonder what happened to the paintings that were hanging in here."

The entrance hall looked yellowed in the lamplight, but every inch of it was spotlessly clean. For that reason the lighter patches on the walls where a number of large paintings had been hung were obvious. The floor under our feet was highly polished wood.

"I'll bet the house goes to one heir, and the furnishings to one or more of the others," Nolan said, answering his own question. "That has to be why the paintings were removed—to get them ready to be taken away. You know, I think that wallpaper and the carpeting were made looking faded. It all sort of blends in with the atmosphere of this place—colorless old age."

"That was the way Mrs. Allyn preferred it," a female voice said, and we turned to see the woman in the doorway to the right of the stairs. "Knowing her husband was dying took the life out of her. And she was color-blind, so to her one shade was as good as another. But Mrs. Allyn did love this house, just the way the rest of us who lived here did."

The words were reasonably mild, but there had been reproof in the woman's tone. And hurt—definitely hurt.

"I didn't mean to sound as though I were criticizing," my companion apologized immediately. "I'm James Nolan, Miss Tappan's financial adviser, and this, of course, is Carrie Tappan."

"And I'm Mrs. Haines," the woman said with a warm smile for me as she stepped forward. "I sent Daniel out the side door to get your bags, and he'll put them in the proper rooms. I'll introduce you to our other guests, Miss Tappan, then you and Mr. Nolan can freshen up before dinner."

I smiled my thanks, at the same time looking the woman over. Her manner suggested that she wouldn't have seemed out of place in a neat print dress down to her ankles, a fluffy white apron around her waist and a wooden spoon still coated with chocolate icing in her hand. More accurately, her dress was knee-length and deep blue, with a small amount of white lace at the rounded collar and cuffs. Her hair was short and brown and her brown eyes were filled with intelligence, but I couldn't get over the impression that she seemed ready to mother the universe.

Mrs. Haines led the way to the left of the stairs, where a hallway stretched between two walls with doors in them. "Back there and to the other side of the stairs are the kitchen and rear porch, the pantry, and servants' quarters," she said, gesturing in that direction. "The first door off the hall on the other side is the dining room, and beyond it the room that was Mr. Allyn's study. On this side the first room is the ballroom, and beyond it is the front parlor. There's another parlor at the end of the hall upstairs to the left, and a billiards room at the end to the right. The billiards room is also the smoking room. If you'd like a tour of the house tomorrow, I'll be glad to have someone show you around."

"Thank you," I murmured, and Nolan said something to the same effect. She'd sounded so sad making that offer, as though she couldn't have given us the tour herself without crying.

"The others should be in here," she told us, and opened the fourth door on the left. Inside was a large room with chairs and couches and tables arranged in sedate groupings. The bare walls had the same light patches that the entrance hall did, and everything in the room was overstuffed and in shades of either gold or brown. If the air-conditioning hadn't been going full blast it would have been hard to breathe.

The three people in the room didn't seem to share my feelings, though. A woman was seated in a wing chair not far from where two men stood. The two had been looking through the light-gold curtains to the veranda beyond the French doors, but when we walked inside they all looked in our direction.

"Our fourth, at last!" one of the men announced, coming forward with a grin. "We're finally ready to get started."

"Really, Brent, you're making it sound like a game of bridge," the woman said with a tinkling laugh. "I'm sure we're all expecting much more than bridge winnings."

"I'd like to introduce Miss Carrie Tappan, and her financial adviser, Mr. James Nolan," Mrs. Haines interrupted. The banter didn't seem to amuse her; she acted as if she hadn't heard it. "Miss Tappan, that gentleman is Brent Lawler, the young lady is Leslie Allyn and the other gentleman is Jeff Allyn. Dinner will be at seven, as usual, so please do be prompt."

Mrs. Haines directed her last words to all of us then left the room, quietly closing the door behind her.

"Yes, Mommy," Brent Lawler's voice murmured wryly. With dark hair and green eyes, he was almost as handsome as James Nolan, especially when he smiled. He wore designer jeans, looked broad shouldered in a long-sleeved sports shirt in green, white and gray, and his sneakers were almost new.

"Don't take it so personally, Brent," Leslie Allyn said with a laugh as she rose gracefully from her chair. "Mrs. Haines is trying to coax us all out of being vultures and wastrels. But speaking for myself, I love being a wastrel."

She stopped next to Brent Lawler with a highly amused look on her beautiful face. Long auburn hair and bright violet eyes made her someone who would stand out in any crowd. She had graceful, long-fingered hands, and wore an expensive slacks-and-shirt outfit in a soft cream, which showed off her slender but well-rounded body without actually showing it. Her shoes had only medium-high heels, but she was tall enough not to need more height.

"*I'm* not a wastrel," the second man, Jeff Allyn, said as he joined us. "At least, I've never had enough money to qualify as one, but I'm more than willing for that to change."

His grin made his gray eyes dance as he shared the joke with Leslie. Tall and dark-haired, and just as broad-shouldered as Brent Lawler, he was handsome, definitely handsome. That made three handsome men I couldn't do anything about. When I saw Miller Houston again, I'd probably kill him.

"Leslie Allyn and Jeff Allyn," Nolan mused to my left. "Does that make you two brother and sister, or husband and wife?"

"It makes us cousins," Leslie answered as she let her gaze move slowly over Nolan. "My father and Jeff's are brothers to Uncle Desmond, and Brent's mother is his sister. For some reason he left nothing to his siblings, only to their firstborn children. I have two younger sisters and a brother, but none of them were mentioned in the will, either."

"My brother didn't like that at all," Jeff Allyn said with another grin. "He's always insisted I got more of what there was to get, and now he feels he can prove it. What about you, pretty lady? Aren't you from Aunt Rebecca's side of the family?"

"Yes. Yes, I am," I answered, trying not to notice the appreciative way his gray eyes studied me. "And I don't have any brothers or sisters."

"Lucky as well as pretty," Brent Lawler said. "But actually, we're the lucky ones. If Aunt Rebecca hadn't killed herself just as Uncle Desmond was dying, his entire estate would have gone to her. And since she didn't have a will, Carrie's father would have inherited as Rebecca's only surviving relative."

"You sound as if you've been studying the matter," Nolan told him in an interested way. "Are you a lawyer, or do you do that sort of thing as a hobby?"

"I do that sort of thing when I'm personally involved," Brent answered with a small laugh. "As for being a lawyer, that's the only bar I'm *not* a member of. I have an import business that takes my attention every now and then, and one of the things I handle is fine wines. May I offer you a sample, Carrie? I brought enough with me for all of us to party."

"The child might not be old enough to drink, but I believe Mr. Nolan is," Leslie put in before I could accept or refuse. "Would you like to get *me* a glass of wine, Mr. Nolan, or are you . . . otherwise engaged?"

"A glass of wine?" Nolan echoed with a faint smile. "Of course. And Carrie is old enough to do anything she cares to. Which way to your supply, Mr. Lawler?"

"This way, and call me 'Brent'" was the quietly amused answer.

They walked off toward the left side of the room while Nolan offered his own first name. Very frankly, I couldn't think of a thing to say. Jim Nolan had defended me against Leslie's snide remark, and Brent Lawler was giving him clear approval for doing it. Nolan had also brushed off Leslie's pass, which had taken the smile from her face and sent her a few angry paces toward the veranda doors. Jeff Allyn glanced at her, then stepped a bit closer to me.

"Not to change the subject from wine, but I hope you're not bothered by thunderstorms," he said with an easy smile. "When you walked in, Brent and I were trying to decide when the storm would hit. If you are bothered, though, please don't hesitate to call on me. I have a lot of pull with thunderstorms."

"Why?" I asked. "Are you a weatherman?"

"No, I'm not a meteorologist, I'm a chemist," he answered with a delighted laugh. "What I meant was that I've always liked thunderstorms, so they and I get along. If you need someone to put in a good word, just remember I'm that someone."

"I'll keep it in mind," I muttered, forcing myself to look away from him. I didn't want to look away, any more than I wanted to ignore Jim Nolan or refuse Brent Lawler's wine. In fact, I would have enjoyed handing out numbers, but I was there to do a job.

Jeff had just begun saying something else, when the other two men came back, Jim with two glasses of wine, Brent with three. Jim was polite when he handed one of his glasses to Leslie, but Brent was downright courtly when he gave one to me. Jeff got the second glass of the three, nodded his thanks and then grinned.

"You look like you're about to kiss her hand, Brent," he remarked. "If you do, just remember that you also gave me a glass. I'm a strong believer in equality."

"I like you, Jeff, but not *that* much," Brent responded with a laugh. "Sorry to tell you this, but I prefer blondes."

"So do I, and I saw her first," Jim Nolan put in as he returned from his chore. "You two gentlemen *are* going to be gentlemen about this?"

"There's a difference between a gentleman and a fool," Jeff told him affably. "I believe in being reasonable, but..."

By then I had slipped back from them, and was glancing around for signs of whoever was directing that comedy. I mean, was I really supposed to believe all that? Three incredibly attractive men, a beautiful woman like Leslie, and all three men were after *me?* I might be pretty, but pretty wasn't enough to explain what was happening. Something was definitely going on, but was it my place to find out what? I was just there to claim an inheritance for a client.

"Men are disgusting, aren't they?" Leslie's soft voice asked suddenly from my right.

"Well, you know two of them better than I do," I returned just as softly. "Are they always like that?"

"I don't know them that much better," she answered scornfully. "The three of us met here for the first time, loving members of a loving family that spread out to hell and gone. Watching them act like that, I'm glad it did."

"Aunt Rebecca and Uncle Desmond never had any children of their own," I said, looking down at the sparkling burgundy in my glass. "Maybe that's why we're here now, the firstborns of their brothers and sisters. We represent the children they never had."

"Even though they never really met any of us?" she asked. "Well, maybe that's the best way to have children. Pick them out and then let somebody else raise them. I may try that someday. Right now even surrogate children would cramp my style."

I studied her face. She seemed to be in her early twenties; her two cousins appeared to be in their late twenties to early thirties. The discrepancy in their ages struck me as odd. "Your father is the eldest now that Uncle Desmond is gone?"

"Oh, Uncle Desmond wasn't the eldest," she began, then abruptly cut off her words with a dazzling smile. "Not that it matters. I find family details *so* boring. If you aren't going to drink that wine, I'll be glad to take it off your hands."

Since burgundy has never been one of my favorites, I gave her my glass to replace the one she'd just about emptied. I was tempted to ask how old she really was, but that might have been out of character. It was funny that, like me, she looked younger than she was, but to her it was no problem. Men with money often preferred youth to maturity, and hadn't she said something about enjoying being a wastrel?

I sighed quietly as I turned away from her, congratulating myself on deducing that her father was the eldest, although that didn't necessarily mean she had to be as old or older than her cousins, not when her father might have taken his time getting married. The guesswork was a warmup for tackling another question, the one posed by the three men still in the midst of amiable conversation. Three very attractive men, and all of them chasing little ol' me....

No, they weren't chasing *me*—that was the answer. They were chasing Carrie Tappan, a young lady they all seemed to know about. The only daughter of a wealthy, influential man of affairs, the girl would make an excellent catch for a struggling importer or chemist, or for a man who had broken with his own wealthy family. And that didn't even take into consideration what Carrie would inherit when the will was read. The slender ghost of a girl who was the real Carrie would probably have been overwhelmed by the largesse... maybe I'd judged her mother's decision a little too harshly.

"Excuse the interruption," a bored voice said, and I turned to the corridor door to see Daniel. Beside him was a woman in a decidedly low-cut maid's uniform, who didn't seem to mind that he was doing the talking. "If Miss Tappan and Mr. Nolan would like to see their rooms now, we're here to show them the way."

"Yes, I *would* like to see my room," I said before Jim Nolan could decide differently for both of us. I also wanted to be alone for a little while, to do some thinking.

"Freshening up a bit sounds good," Nolan commented, finishing his wine and putting the glass aside. "Not to mention the fact that my clothes will enjoy being unpacked."

"Come on, then," Daniel said, turning from the doorway without waiting to see if we really were ready to follow just that instant. His attitude was beginning to annoy me, but it wasn't something to make a fuss about under those circumstances.

"I'll see you later, Carrie," Brent called as I walked out just ahead of Nolan. I pretended not to hear him and simply kept going.

"Daniel, I'm told the only phone in the house is in Mr. Allyn's study," Nolan said as we followed the boy back toward the entrance hall. "Is there some set procedure for using the thing, or should we simply go in and help ourselves?"

"The study door is left open when no one's on the phone," Daniel responded with a glance back at us. "If the door's closed, someone is in there and you have to wait your turn."

"I'll probably take advantage of that a little later," Nolan said with a nod, then the subject was dropped.

We followed our two guides up those beautiful stairs to the second floor, and Daniel took Nolan to the right, while the maid led me to the left. The upper hallway was fairly wide, with three doors on each side of what must have been the master suite in the middle. There was also another set of three doors to the left of the ones beside the master suite, facing the front of the house. Straight ahead, at the end of the hall, was what had to be the second-floor parlor. We passed the first sets of doors, then turned in toward the third door on the right.

"This one is yours, Miss," the girl told me quietly as we walked in. For someone who showed so much cleavage, she was almost as shy as Carrie. "Miss Allyn is in the first room on the other side of the hall, so neither of you will disturb the other. I unpacked your bags and put everything away, but if you don't like the arrangement I'll redo it. Your bath is in there, through the door on the right."

"I'm sure everything will be fine," I told her with a faint smile. "Thank you."

"My pleasure, Miss," she answered with a return smile. "I'm Megin, and if you need me just pull the bell cord."

"Thank you, Megin," I repeated, then turned to look at the room again after she'd closed the door behind her. The wide canopied, curtained bed to the left was the most imposing feature, but the beautifully carved writing desk and big black leather armchair tied for second place. The sliding doors of the closet were just beyond the bathroom door to the right, and straight ahead were veranda doors with drapes matching the bed curtains. Both were a filmy white with a muted design in red, tan, brown and black, and the pure white bed linen was scattered with throw pillows in the same colors. The carpeting was tan and very soft, and the wall switch had turned on a porcelain desk lamp.

"And this air-conditioning is starting to make me wish for a coat," I muttered, rubbing my arms with both hands. "I wonder what those three would have done if I'd asked for a volunteer to help keep me warm."

Since I could almost see them scrambling to be first, I smiled as I walked to the armchair and sat. I'd always been something of a believer in poetic justice, but now I was sold on the idea. Carrie Tappan had been forced to give up a lot in her life, but because of that had escaped the possibility of falling in love with a man who had no real interest in her. Was there anything worse than loving a man who wanted something other than you?

I couldn't think of much worse, but I could see where the next couple of days might turn out to be interesting. Carrie would never have been able to cope with those three characters, but I was only using her name. Underneath I was still Ann Mellion, and the tomboy in me had a sense of humor. Was there any reason not to share it with the three charming gentlemen pursuing an heiress?

As long as I did it in character, no reason at all. I smiled again as I let my hands slide over the smooth leather of the chair arms, enjoying its faint scent. Miller would have a fit if he found out, but who was going to tell him?

I wondered then if I should call Miller about the incident at the airport. Nolan's suggestion of mistaken identity could be true, but it was also possible that the incident had been staged so that I might be rescued by a fearless hero. Since the chauffeur had been anxious to get me out of the airport as fast as possible, chances were that the rescue was scheduled for later on at another location. That meant any of the three could have set it up....

But it hadn't worked. I got out of the chair again and went toward the bathroom, suddenly deciding on a bath. Planning was easier when my body was soaking in hot, soapy water, and I wanted the kidnap plotter to regret his actions. Of course, I still had to find out which one was responsible, but all three of them deserved whatever I dreamed up. It could even turn out to be fun....

WHEN HE FOUND the study empty, he closed the door before going to sit behind the desk near the phone. Rotary phones were a pain, but Desmond Allyn had been one of those ridiculous eccentrics who clung to the past.

"Yeah, it's me," he said when he heard the voice at the other end. "I only have a minute or two, but I wanted you to know that I'm hard at work. She's prettier than I expected, but she's too shy to really know it. Once I turn it on full blast, she'll drag *me* to bed."

The voice at the other end spoke, causing him to grin.

"No, you don't have to worry about that," he said, amusement in his light eyes. "I won't touch her until she promises to marry me, and I'll get that promise on tape. If Daddy tries to break it off, he'll have a breach-of-promise suit on his hands. And by then she'll be willing to testify for *me*."

The voice spoke again, this time making him laugh.

"But of course I'm counting chickens," he answered. "No chicken I've ever come across has refused to be counted, and little Carrie chicken will be no different. I intend getting a rich wife out of this waste of time, and after a year or two I'll have a rich *ex*-wife. I'll also have made a lot of important contacts, which will last well beyond the divorce. I'm telling you, hon, I've got it made."

The voice spoke for the third time, and his smile turned sly.

"You're right, baby, *we've* got it made," he said in a smooth, caressing voice. "You'll be going all the way with me, and after the divorce I'll want a *real* wife. You won't regret waiting. But I've got to go now—I can't afford to be late for dinner."

He exchanged goodbyes and hung up, laughed aloud softly, then left the study.

WHEN HE FOUND the study empty, he closed the door before going to sit behind the desk near the phone. He hadn't seen a rotary phone since his last trip to Europe, and for a while that trip *would* be his last. When things worked out the way they were supposed to, he would be too involved to travel.

"Yes, it's me," he said when a voice answered. "You'd better be ready to explain what went wrong at the airport this afternoon."

The other voice began speaking immediately, but he listened for only a short while before interrupting.

"That's nothing but a string of excuses!" he said in a harsh, low voice. "If we'd taken her then and there, I could have kept my cover character out of it. Now I'll have to get personally involved. It's a good thing for you that I planned for the possibility."

Again the other voice spoke, this time going on a little longer. The man at the desk nodded, his light eyes gleaming.

"That's more like it," he said at last. "Multiple plans in case the first doesn't work. I made contact with our inside plant, but didn't like the way it went. If that turns out to be our weak link, we'll have to eliminate it. I have no patience for weakness."

The voice on the other end asked a question, and the man smiled mirthlessly.

"Yes, I've started to get close to our target, and she and I will turn out to be *very* close. A silly little bit of fluff, but at least she won't give us any trouble once we have her. You get here as soon as you can, and start putting those plans into effect. The next time it's done, I want it done *right*."

He hung up with forceful reassurance ringing in his ears, and that made him feel slightly better. Sweet, pretty little Carrie Tappan. He'd enjoy it when she found out the truth and then he'd enjoy *her.* It was the least she owed him for the trouble he was being put to.

He smiled happily for a moment, then got up and left the room.

WHEN HE FOUND the study empty, he closed the door before going to sit behind the desk near the phone. He was more agitated than he thought he would be. In fact, he was downright angry. He dialed the number quickly, then waited impatiently for someone to answer.

"It's me," he said as soon as he heard acknowledgment at the other end. "Are all you people asleep, or just dead from the neck up?"

There was surprise from the other voice, along with protestations of innocence.

"Don't give me that," he snapped softly, knowing better than to believe them. "Why wasn't I told that the Carrie Tappan making this trip would really be Ann Mellion? When I first saw her, I almost lost it."

Soothing tones now emanated from the receiver, glib excuses as to why it had been for his own good. He listened briefly, light eyes filled with anger, and then he interrupted.

"What you really mean is that you knew I'd never let her walk into this mess blindfolded!" he growled. "Tell me she knows what's happening, that she's ready to defend herself. They think she's their target, so they'll be going after her with everything they have. She—"

The other person interrupted, and the words made him frown. He heard them out, then shook his head.

"The fact that they tried for her at the airport and missed doesn't mean a thing," he disagreed. "She's too much of a professional to break character, not when she doesn't know what's happening. If she couldn't have freed herself while staying in her role, she might have decided to let herself be taken. And why weren't you able to grab the character who tried for her? Or did you tag him and then follow to see where he went?"

More words followed, all of them adding up to the same thing.

"So our people at the airport lost him in the crowds," he summed up in disgust. "Good job they did there, pal. Would they have tried a little harder if he'd managed to hang on to the girl, or would it have been the same story? I'm telling you right now—"

The voice on the other end was tinged with impatience and anger now. It went on for a short while, then stopped to give him the chance to answer.

"You're right and you're wrong," he said after a moment, clearly fighting to keep his temper. "Yes, I do consider that she saved my life, but that doesn't mean I'm ready to betray the department. Didn't I follow orders and stay away from her, when the more I learned about her the more I wanted to give my thanks in person? It was too much of a risk, you said. She couldn't be relied on not to recognize me at the wrong time and place, you said. I went along with all that, but her life wasn't in danger. How can it betray the operation if she's simply told what she's facing?"

The voice took on a faint edge of persuasiveness, but didn't lose the cold tone of command. He sighed and leaned back in his chair, then shook his head.

"I'm not saying I consider a virtual stranger more important than my country's needs," he responded flatly. "I know this job has to be done, and I'm just disagreeing with the way you want to do it. Hasn't it occurred to you that Ann would be an asset to our side? Her security clearance is high enough right now, so what could you—"

A quick interruption conveyed surprise and sudden interest.

"Of course I checked her clearance," he answered with a snort. "I check on every woman I send flowers to anonymously. One of the people in my department did it, to ensure that I wasn't being set up. That was just before your order to stay away came through, so if you like you can check it yourself."

Thoughtful agreement, the sound of scribbling, and then a final order came next.

"All right, I won't give the show away until I hear from you," he said grudgingly. "But that doesn't mean I won't be keeping a close eye on her. It stands to reason that someone here is in on the deal, and if I can catch them in the act we'll have all the answers we need. How will you get in touch with me?"

There was a pause, then the words of a decision.

"Okay, that should work," he agreed. "But don't take too long. The competition is guaranteed to move as fast as they can."

He hung up the phone still not quite trusting what he'd been told. Interagency politics were unbelievably ridiculous; he'd been their victim more than once. Other agencies wanted to borrow his talents, but they still treated him like a spy in their midst. No one watching would ever believe they all worked for the same country.

But it was one thing to sacrifice *him* on the altar of suspicion; he wasn't about to let the same thing be done to Ann. Or Tommy, as a number of her co-workers called her. He really shouldn't have done that much checking on her, but not being allowed to get it firsthand from her...

And now he was right there in the same house with her. He couldn't tell her it was him and she was pretending to be someone else, but there they were...and it was part of his job to make sure she was all right.

He grinned faintly before getting out of the chair, realizing his plans had long since been made. Any of the others could be the one they were after, so in all good conscience he couldn't let any of them get closer to her than he did. Didn't it follow that the closer he was, the better protection he could offer? And in this situation she needed the protection, just the way he'd needed it when she'd drawn deadly fire to give him the chance to keep his life.

After all the smoke settled they might turn out to dislike each other, but that was something they were entitled to find out together. And they'd have the chance—damn every government agency in the book if they didn't. If it really became necessary he'd warn her, no matter what. He left the room, having only a small idea of how determined he looked.

Chapter Four

I made sure to be dressed in time to go down to dinner early. It would be out of character for me to forget about calling my "mother," and before dinner ought to be the best moment.

It had started to rain, which made the heavy humidity worse. I'd tried to open a window to escape the very efficient chill of the air-conditioning, and that was when the weight and wet of the outdoors had hit. I had the choice of freezing or wilting, but only until I left my room. After that it was nothing but icebox.

Or mausoleum, I thought as I walked down the stairs. There wasn't a sound in the whole house suggesting another living being, and the dim light combined with the cool had me thinking about coffins in the basement. As a vacation this experience was missing something, but I didn't expect Miller to believe me. He had trouble believing anything he didn't want to hear.

The hallway behind the dining room and the study felt longer than the one leading to the front parlor. It also seemed darker but the third door to the right stood open, emitting a feeble stream of light. When I reached it I saw I'd found the study, so I went in and closed the door behind me. As thick as those doors and walls were, closing up the room probably made it all but soundproof.

Another door stood open in the wall to the right, and walking over to it showed it led directly into the dining room. The long table was already set with five places, so that meant I didn't have much time. I closed that door as well, and headed for the desk.

Empty shelves lined the walls, speaking of once-beloved books now packed away for disposal. I hate the sight of empty bookshelves as much as the thought of empty minds, one usually being the cause of the other. Aware that the atmosphere of the place was distracting me from what I was supposed to do, I ignored the almost-naked desk and sat down near the phone. A rotary phone. Great.

I dialed Miller's private number carefully, but wasn't sure I'd done it right until I heard his voice. He didn't answer with a name, of course, not in our business.

"Hello, Mother, it's me," I said, automatically using Carrie's soft tones. "The flight was fine, and we got here before the rain started."

"Well, I'm certainly relieved to hear that," Miller returned primly. "I'm assuming you consider the line secure. Is it a private line, or did you do something to the extensions?"

"It's the only line, and there are no extensions," I answered. "Uncle Desmond didn't like things that were too up-to-date, but at least he wasn't a complete fanatic. People who want to use a phone take turns on this one."

"That should make things even easier for you," he said with satisfaction. "Tomorrow the lawyer arrives and reads the will, and as soon as it's over you're on the way home. Don't forget to call me from the airport. If this situation I'm keeping an eye on breaks suddenly, there may not be time for you to stop at home."

"If you can put someone else on that fascinating emergency, you'd better do it," I advised, suddenly feeling highly annoyed. "My traveling companion will probably insist on seeing me right to the door, which is not the only thing I expect him to insist on. And if you can believe it, he's not the only one. We both overlooked the fact that I'm a very eligible young lady, at least as far as the male population in this house is concerned."

"That's James Nolan and who else?" Miller asked after muttering something. "Don't forget you can't encourage any of that, no matter how tempting. Our client will have a fit if word of the substitution gets out, and if any of them try to follow you home and see you again..."

"Yes, I know," I conceded with a sigh. "That would be the end of our reputation for discretion. But you can stop pressing the panic button. I find nothing attractive about men who chase women for their money, no matter how handsome they are. I'll handle them, one way or another."

"Give me the other names," Miller repeated.

"Brent Lawler and Jeff Allyn. They and their cousin Leslie Allyn are the other heirs, but they seem to think they won't be getting much. I wonder what they know that I don't."

"As long as that topic covers nothing but the inheritance, wonder away," Miller offered with typical generosity. "For everything else, those three are strictly off-limits. Our clients are entitled to be considered before any personal feelings."

"Since I wasn't arguing, why are you making such a point of it?" I asked, certain I already knew the answer. "Have you forgotten it's Carrie Tappan they want, not just any handy blonde?"

"You're more than any handy blonde, and I don't want to see you getting hurt," he answered, his tone not just sincere but downright solemn. "I sometimes find myself thinking of you as a daughter, Ann, which has never happened to me before. Are you going to blame me for being concerned?"

"Of course not," I said. "It's just—"

"There goes my other line," he interrupted, suddenly all business again. "I'll see you in a couple of days, and we can continue this discussion then. In the meantime, if you need any help shaking loose, just call and say so."

The click in my ear signaled an end to the conversation. I leaned forward and replaced the receiver, overriding the urge to slam it down hard.

I leaned back in the comfortable chair, looking around at the empty, forlorn room. All decoration had been taken from the walls, shelves, and tables, leaving behind nothing but the bare bones of one-time warmth. Right then I felt exactly like the room, stripped and vulnerable, uncertain about what the future would bring.

"I sometimes find myself thinking of you as a daughter," Miller had said. As if he had no idea my parents were half a world away and that, when I stopped to remember that fact, I missed them terribly. Archaeologists don't do well in providing a stable home for more than a few months out of the year, especially if they're a husband-and-wife team with the sort of credentials others dream about. But when they're wonderful people who are very much in love, those few months can be better than full-time in another family. My sister and I had never felt cheated, only disappointed when it became time for Mrs. Ryan to come back to take care of us.

But Miller had apparently decided I needed a father image to replace my actual father. You don't disagree with a father image the way you do with an employer, and you don't get involved with men who haven't been given his approval.

I swore under my breath, then tried to consider the matter objectively. It was possible that Miller hadn't been lying to rope me in more tightly, but if that was true, why had he called me "Ann"? Because I'd told him I didn't want to be called "Tommy," or because he'd gone overboard trying to sound sincere?

In all honesty I had to admit that Miller could be sincere, even though I was still suspicious. We'd worked together for more than five years, and you develop feelings of family in that amount of time. The fact that he'd been giving me more and more to do either meant that he appreciated just how good I was and was taking advantage of it, or he was simply trying to help guarantee my success in the business. Either way...

Either way it wasn't something that I had to worry about right then and there. The problem of Miller Houston could wait until I was back in D.C., and that left only the problem of dinner. Starving to death was close to what I felt, so it was more than time to join the others. I opened the door to the hallway and left it open, then used the door leading into the dining room.

Jim Nolan and Brent Lawler stood to the far left of the room near a short bar, drinks in hand as they talked. Jim was still wearing the suit he'd traveled in, but Brent had changed from his jeans to a suit. With the table and the rest of the room between us they didn't notice me at first, but Jeff Allyn took care of that. Also dressed in a suit and tie, he appeared in the doorway opposite the one I'd used only a moment earlier, and immediately came toward me with a big smile.

"No one can tell me this doesn't mean something significant," he said by way of greeting. "You and me arriving at the same time—it has to be fate. Has anyone ever told you how beautiful you look in pale pink?"

By then he was really too close, and his smile had widened into a faint grin. I sincerely doubted that fate had had a hand with the timing he'd mentioned, but didn't intend to say so. There were much better things to say, and he was my first victim.

"Oh, yes, lots of people have told me I look nice in pink," I answered with a dismissive smile. "Do you happen to know how close we are to eating? I'm really very hungry."

"I suppose we're just waiting for Leslie," he said with a quick glance around, and then the smile was back. "I hope you'll do me the honor of sitting next to me during dinner. Then I won't care whether the food is good or bad."

"*I'll* care," I responded, promptly making myself look worried. "You don't think it *will* be bad, do you? I mean, I'm sure all of us are hungry..."

"Now, this isn't fair, Jeff," Brent said as he and Jim came up, mild scolding in his tone. "Keeping this lovely creature all to yourself won't be tolerated, at least not by me. There are certain things a true gentleman won't do."

"Like what?" Jim asked, definite amusement in his light eyes. "And didn't someone mention earlier the difference between being a gentleman and being a fool?"

"Brent is just upset because Carrie has agreed to sit beside me during dinner," Jeff said. "If he'd been lucky enough to see her first, he would have gotten to ask first."

"But I'm the one who really saw her first," Jim pointed out. "Since no one can argue that, I think Carrie ought to sit beside me."

"Have I mentioned that my health has been poor lately?" Brent asked, coughing as he pounded on his chest with a fist. "Since I may not be long for this world, I think it's only fair if Carrie sits with me."

The other two laughed as they booed his acting and outrageous lying, and I couldn't help wondering how I would feel if I thought they were truly interested. When a man looks directly at you as Jeff had at me, his eyes telling you you're the only sight they're interested in seeing, when he makes a truly pitiful effort to get your sympathy as Brent had, or when he announces happily that *he* saw you first, as Jim had...

But they weren't seriously interested, not in me and not in the real Carrie Tappan. They were out to take advantage of a shy, inexperienced girl who would be overwhelmed by the attention; shooting fish in a barrel would be more sporting, but they didn't care. They were going ahead with their plans, which meant I would be going ahead with mine.

"Excuse me," a voice said, interrupting the friendly wrangling. We all turned to see Mrs. Haines, warm and homey in her white-trimmed blue dress. "We're ready to serve dinner, but Miss Allyn isn't here. I tapped at her door and peeked into the room, but she wasn't there, either. Have any of you seen her?"

"Miss Tappan and I haven't seen her since we went up to our rooms," Jim offered. "Maybe Mr. Lawler or Mr. Allyn have her stashed away somewhere."

"I went up to change shortly after you two did," Jeff said promptly, quick to clear himself of the "stashing" charge. "That leaves you, Brent. What have you done with the poor girl?"

"Nothing I can remember, and I usually have a good memory for things like that," Brent answered with a grin. "She was drinking wine and looking out at the rain when I left, but I had the impression she wouldn't stay there long. Maybe she changed her mind and lost track of the time."

"That could be it," Jeff agreed, then turned back to Mrs. Haines. "Have you looked in the parlor?"

"No," she responded, but now that she'd been given a direction she took it.

None of the others seemed interested in following until I did, then they trooped along behind without comment. If Leslie was deliberately delaying her appearance in order to make an entrance or a point, I wanted to know it. If there was some other reason...

Mrs. Haines opened the parlor door and walked in, then stopped short with a sound of distress. Leslie Allyn sat sprawled in a chair, her glass held so loosely that the wine in it had spilled onto the carpeting. Her head lolled to one side, her eyes were closed, and the sound of snoring came from between slackly parted lips.

"Would you call that a testimonial to my wares?" Brent asked, his tone wry. "If I'd known she had a problem, I wouldn't have left her alone with temptation."

"It could be she just got bored and overdid it," Jim suggested. "How many did she have before Carrie and I got here?"

"None of us had much," Jeff said, "but I wasn't really counting. Or watching her, for that matter. I think we ought to put her to bed."

"And forget about mentioning this tomorrow," Jim added as Brent began to move toward her with Jeff. "However it happened, she won't enjoy being reminded about it."

"I second that," Brent said, giving us all a quick glance. "There's no reason to bring up things people do by accident."

"Which we all know is what happened here," Jeff put in, making the decision unanimous. "You get her arms, Brent, and I'll take her legs."

After freeing the wineglass from her hand, Brent fought his half of Leslie out of the chair. Jeff had a good grip on her legs, but the two men weren't having an easy time of it. The girl was completely limp, a dead weight that bent in the wrong places and at odd angles. When they almost dropped her, Jim hurried forward.

"I'd better give you a hand," he said, putting his arms more or less around her waist. "Mrs. Haines, will you open doors for us?"

The dark-haired woman had looked concerned about the wine stain on the carpeting, but with her people did come first. She began to lead the way back toward the stairs with a minimum of fluttering upset, and the three men carried their burden after her. I waited a moment to be sure they were gone, then I went over to the collection of bottles Brent Lawler had brought.

It hadn't been possible to be certain from a distance, but up close there was no question. Behind a number of clean glasses were fifteen wine bottles, apparently from every country in Europe but France. One bottle had been completely emptied and put to the back and a second was more than two-thirds gone, but the rest were still corked. Not even two bottles had been finished.

"Which means she isn't drunk," I said under my breath, suddenly very uneasy. I didn't like what I was starting to think, but there *was* a way to double-check. The glass Leslie had used was on the small table where Brent had left it, and that was my next stop. Sniffing gave me no more than the faintest of hints, but a tiny taste of the last drop left unspilled made my tongue feel spiked.

"And 'spiked' is the proper word," I muttered, putting the glass back. Something had been slipped into Leslie's wine, and while I wasn't sure which drug it was, I had no doubt about its being there. Knockout drops, intended to put her fast asleep.

But why? I looked around the empty room. Why would anyone want to drug Leslie, not to poison her but to put her to sleep? It made no sense, even if she turned out to be the heir who got the most. Being asleep would not keep her from inheriting, and if she had died in that sleep, there would be the investigation that proved only a few of us had had access to the wine. No, it had to be something else.

I stopped short in my roaming around the room, having realized that I still had the scent of burgundy wine in my nostrils. Burgundy, the wine I disliked, a glass of which I had given to Leslie without having tasted it.

So the knockout drops had probably been meant for me. I walked over to the curtained veranda doors and looked out, seeing little of the evening dimness or the pouring rain. My mind had gone into a frenzy of guesswork, formulating possibilities and discarding half of them, jumping around like a frightened frog. If it had been me who had swallowed that wine, *I'd* now be the one lying unconscious and helpless.

But why? That afternoon at the airport and the incident with the chauffeur I could understand as being part of a plan to impress me, but drugged wine didn't make sense. Unless one of them had intended being in my bed when I awoke, claiming I'd invited him and that we were now engaged....

Something like that was possible, but it still didn't feel quite right. In a situation like that Carrie Tappan might simply agree, but she also might go into hysterics. Either the one behind the ploy had no real idea of the girl he was dealing with, or... Or I was reading the whole thing wrong. Could the two incidents be separate, with two different men behind them?

But that made things even worse! How was I supposed to avoid disaster if two of these men really were willing to go to such lengths? Either I stayed in character and let it happen, or I betrayed the trust of a client and defended myself the right way. Assuming I could decide which ones to defend myself against, or which one if there was only one.

Filled with the most peculiar feeling, I turned away from the window and rubbed my arms. I'd never worried about being alone with a man, knowing that nothing would happen that I couldn't handle. Now I was virtually alone with three men, and had no idea which way to turn. Things would have to get really desperate before I betrayed a client.

Which meant I would continue to be a sitting duck for three fortune hunters. If one of them did something I didn't care for, I'd have to slap his face rather than break his arm. Gad! How did other women go through life like that?

Nervously was the obvious answer, just the way *I* felt. A dim room like that parlor wasn't soothing or romantic; it was a trap for the spider who was trying to pull me into his web. Or maybe there were two or three spiders, each weaving his own web. All three of the men had had access to my glass of wine: Brent and Jim when they'd gone to get it, Jeff while he'd stood so close beside me. How was I supposed to figure out who the culprit was?

I began to pace. I should be out of that house by the following afternoon at the latest, but in the meanwhile it would hurt nothing to try to get some answers. I could talk to the three men separately, providing them the chance to say something that would give them away. Maybe in alphabetical order...

"Oh!" I yelped when the hand touched my shoulder. I whirled around, heart pounding and expecting the worst.

Jeff was immediately apologetic. "I'm sorry, Carrie, I didn't mean to frighten you," he said, his gray eyes serious. "This place is so gloomy it would be enough to scare Bela Lugosi. Here, let me hold you for a moment."

"No, no, I'm fine, thank you." I gulped, stepping back from his arms. This was my chance to start questioning, and it would be in reverse alphabetical order....

"Leslie is out to the world, Brent and Jim went back to the dining room and Mrs. Haines is about to serve dinner," Jeff said. He'd looked disappointed when I hadn't let him take me in his arms, but only for a moment. "The others thought they'd find you in the dining room, but I had a hunch and so came back here. Hunches are wonderful things, aren't they?"

His grin, which reached even to his eyes, made his broad face even more attractive. Black hair and gray eyes looked really good on a man, especially when he was also tall and broad-shouldered.

"Is Leslie going to be all right?" I asked, silently snarling at myself. Was I so impressed by a handsome face that this was the best I could come up with?

"She'll probably be fine until she wakes up," he answered, his grin fading. "After that she'll have the dickens of a hangover, which might even be enough to teach her better next time. What's your favorite color?"

"Why would you possibly want to know that?" I asked, suddenly thrown off balance. I'd meant to ask a different question, but with *that* coming out of the blue...

"A man should know such things about a woman," he answered, smiling as he stroked my cheek with the back of one finger. "I'll bet you like blue and green, to match the blue-green of your eyes. Am I right?"

I had to force myself to step back from his touch. Which, under the circumstances, was ridiculous. So what if he was incredibly attractive?

"I live in Washington, D.C.," I blurted, for the first time really thankful that I was supposed to be the shy, inexperienced Carrie. "Where do you live?"

"In Atlanta, Georgia," he answered, obviously amused by the clumsy way I'd changed subjects. "Have you ever been to Atlanta?"

"Once," I ventured. "There was a diplomatic convention of some kind, and I went with my parents. We stayed in the Marriott, across the street from the Vista."

"That's a Hilton across the street from the Marriott," he corrected gently, still amused. "Vista is the name of Hilton's international corporation."

"Oh," I answered, trying to look flustered at my lack of knowledge. "And you're a chemist in Atlanta?"

"Some people say I'd be a chemist anywhere," he returned, the grin widening again. "You know, a chemist is a person who has the talent for turning money into organic fertilizer. Haven't you ever heard that one?"

I shook my head. "You don't sound like you come from Atlanta," I pointed out with exquisite subtlety. "You don't have that lovely accent."

"I do when I forget to watch what I'm saying," he replied. "My job has me traveling around a good deal, and my company thought I'd make a better impression on our customers without a regional accent. That's why I spent time studying speech. Say, I'm sorry. You told me earlier you were hungry, and here I stand bending your ear when food's about to be served. Let's continue this in the dining room."

He took my right arm and wrapped it around his left, and we headed for the dining room. We had run out of conversation, but it's possible I wasn't supposed to notice. It's certain I wasn't supposed to take note of the fact that a chemist would have the most convenient access to knockout drops.

Jim and Brent met us at the foot of the stairs in the entrance hall, obviously on their way to the parlor. Jeff put his right hand on mine to keep me from slipping free of him, and we all returned to the dining room. Mrs. Haines was just coming in through another door, carrying a soup tureen, but she stopped to give us time to reach the table.

"Place cards have been provided to avoid confusion," she said, her tone warm and amused. "Tomorrow at breakfast they'll be arranged differently."

Those were pacifying words if I'd ever heard any, and they probably kept a fight from starting. Brent had been assigned to the head of the table, me to his left and Jim to my left. Leslie was supposed to have been on his right, with Jeff to her right.

"Too bad, Jeffrey old boy," Brent chortled as he stopped behind his chair. "You get to deliver the lady, but you don't get to stay."

"That's 'Jeffers,'" Jeff corrected with an easy laugh. "Jeffers Wayne Allyn, and I will be back. If not sooner, then tomorrow for breakfast."

He walked me to my chair between Brent and Jim, paused to kiss my hand as Jim got to his feet again, then went around to his chair. It took me a moment to realize that they were all waiting for *me* to sit down before they'd do the same, so I did it fast. I usually appreciate good manners in a man, but those three were making it somewhat overwhelming.

The meal started out tasty and went uphill from there. Whoever had done the cooking knew what they were about, and we all stuffed ourselves. Soup, salad, fried chicken, potatoes and peas and corn, fresh bread and lots of butter—we probably gained ten pounds apiece, but it was worth it. The only thing I didn't touch was the wine, asking instead for water or a soft drink. Mrs. Haines brought out a bottle of Dr. Pepper, remarking in passing that Daniel had gotten corrupted by the drink in Texas.

Brent excused himself just before the chicken was brought, Jeff did the same halfway through the meal, and Jim took his turn right after dessert. None of them was gone more than a couple of minutes, but from my end of the table it wasn't possible to see where they went. Upstairs? To the parlor to remove all evidence? To set something else up for later?

Having an unsolved problem doesn't usually affect my appetite, but when dessert—a lovely peach cobbler—was brought, I begged off with the excuse that I was already too stuffed. My companions dug in with enthusiasm, though, but why shouldn't they have? They knew what they'd done when they left the table. I became lost in frustrated thought, and the next thing I knew Mrs. Haines was telling us that coffee would be served in the parlor.

"Well, then, let's get to it," Brent said, using his napkin for the last time before tossing it on the table. "Carrie, my sweet, may I have the honor of escorting you there? You let my cousin Jeff be your escort earlier, and you don't want me think you like him better, do you?''

I parted my lips to answer, just about the first words I'd said during the entire meal, but Jim didn't wait to hear them.

''I'm sorry, Brent, but you'll have to play escort another time,'' he said with a smile. ''I need a few private words with Carrie, then we'll join you and Jeff in the parlor. A business matter, you understand.''

''Yes, and I think I know what kind of business,'' Brent answered with a defeated sigh. ''Well, no sense in being a bad sport. My turn will come.''

He and Jeff left the table with smiles and nods for me, and Jim waited until they were gone before he said, ''Let's go and stand by the windows. There are only a couple of things I want to say, then we'll join them again.''

I let him help me out of the chair, and his hand in my back gently guided me to a place by the veranda doors not far from the short bar. His beautiful smile flashed for me when I glanced at him, so I tried not to glance at him again. It was hell being that close to a man like James Nolan, a tall, handsome, black-haired man with gorgeous blue eyes. I knew I was being a fool again, but I couldn't seem to help it.

''Now no one will overhear us if they happen to come in,'' he said in a soft voice when we stopped. ''Carrie...we haven't known each other very long, have we?''

I looked up to see that he was actually waiting for an answer, so I shook my head. He smiled when I did, and took my right hand in both of his.

''I almost wish we were old friends,'' he said, wistfulness clear in his voice and eyes. ''That would make saying what I have to much easier. Carrie, when you and I first met, I felt something so special I find it impossible to describe. You're sweet and pretty and a lot nicer than a cynical old man like me, and that's why I feel I have to intrude on a part of your life that should be no one's business but yours."

"I—I don't understand," I said, an understatement if ever there was one. His hands held my smaller one as if it were a wild but fragile bird, which wasn't helping.

"Your two undeniably distant cousins," he said with a sad smile. "They came after you the instant we walked in, but I'm very much afraid it isn't your prettiness or niceness they're interested in. They've said in so many words that they have no money, but they both seem to know that you do. Surely your parents have warned you about men who know of your wealth?"

"Well, yes, they have," I admitted, refraining from mentioning someone else who fit that description. "But I find it really hard to believe—"

"Now, wait," he advised. "I'm not saying they *are* the sort we've been discussing, but they could be. All I'd like to ask you to do is not take what they tell you seriously. Enjoy their attention, have fun with it—but if you begin to feel uneasy come and talk to me about it. You know I won't let anything hurt you, and between us we can decide what to do. Will you promise me that?"

"If you like," I agreed, very aware of the way his thumb rubbed back and forth across the top of my fingers.

"That's my good girl," he said with a really devastating smile, then raised my hand to his lips. "Mmm, you taste good. No wonder those two like the idea of hand kissing so much. Do you want to go in for our coffee now?"

"Where—where are you from originally?" I asked as I slid my hand free, not quite avoiding his gaze. He was instantly amused, but didn't say so.

"Washington was my home originally, and now it is again," he answered with nothing more than a smile. "In between I've lived in a lot of places, and even went to school in some of them. My undergraduate degree is from NYU."

"New York University," I ventured, letting him see that I was impressed. "That's supposed to be a very big school. Didn't you want to go to law school there?"

"No, by then I'd decided not to go into law," he reminded me. "And a place like NYU Law School, so big and impersonal—have you ever been to New York?"

I shook my head, and he put an arm around me to start us walking toward the entrance hall.

"Someday I'd like to take you there," he murmured, looking down at me with bright blue eyes. "All the noise and rushing around, the mobs of people. Washington Square Park would be our first stop, to listen to the people making speeches on any number of political or philosophical topics. We could wander through the park for a couple of hours, simply enjoying ourselves, then I'd take you to Broadway. Would you like to see Broadway with me someday, Carrie?"

"Oh, yes," I breathed, and that seemed to satisfy him. He leaned down, brushed my lips with his, and then we went on to the parlor.

"We were about to send a posse with bloodhounds after you two," Brent said when we walked in. "Everything of a business nature all cleared up?"

"For the moment," Jim told him with an agreeable smile. "And now we're ready for our coffee. As quickly as possible, in fact, before I go into total caffeine withdrawal."

"You sound like Jeff," Brent remarked with a laugh. "Personally I've been kicking myself for not bringing any brandy, but I'll make do with the Irish whiskey Uncle Desmond so thoughtfully provided. Anyone else want some?"

Jim and I both refused together, and I had the feeling Jeff had done the same. He sat with his coffee cup not far from where we'd found Leslie, but the glass she'd used was gone. The wine spill on the carpeting had also been mopped up, but there was still enough of a stain to be noticeable.

I watched carefully as Jim poured coffee for both of us, then took the cup he handed me. Cream and sugar were next on the list for his coffee, and I waited patiently until he was through. Letting him drink first was one way to make sure nothing had been added before we arrived. If he took a sip and began to go blurry, I'd know enough to find something else to drink.

Rather than sipping Jim took a good swallow, then *aahed* with satisfaction. The coffee apparently met with his approval, but, then, so had the coffee at the airport. I gave it another thirty seconds, watching him surreptitiously, and then tried a tiny sip of my own. There was no bite even from the coffee, and that made me feel considerably better.

"Carrie, my sweet, I'd like to show you something," Brent murmured from my right. "Will you come with me for just a minute or two? It isn't far."

His left hand took my elbow as he smiled, those green eyes projecting warmth and gentleness. I suddenly discovered I was walking with him without consciously deciding to agree, but I didn't stop. It had gotten to be Brent's turn, and right in the proper order.

He guided me to one of the veranda doors, opened it and urged me out ahead of him. The rain was coming down hard. Beneath the protection of the pillared porch there was no more than mist in the air, but the air itself weighed a ton. I wondered if that sort of leaden humidity was usual for spring in Louisiana, then forgot the question as Brent closed the veranda door behind us.

"Isn't this nice?" he asked, gesturing with his coffee cup. "It's dark and wet out there, but it's also serene and secret. Standing here lets you share that serenity."

It was also giving me a break from the air-conditioning. Just then the warmth of the night felt better than the chill of indoors, and the company wasn't all that bad, either. I sipped again at my coffee, trying to see the rain rather than just hear it, and Brent stirred and sighed.

"Look, I want to say something," he began, as though about to launch into a terrible confession. "I don't feel very good about it, but it does have to be said. You're not like the other women I've met in my life, and it wouldn't be fair to—"

He chopped the sentence off, took a small sip from his Irish coffee, then smiled faintly.

"I never expected this to be so hard," he said, then looked directly at me. "What I'm trying to say, Carrie, is that you shouldn't trust any of us. Not me, not Jeff, not even that business adviser of yours. You haven't known him long, have you?"

He waited for me to shake my head, then showed a cynical smile.

"I thought not," he said, putting his free hand to my hair. "We're all the same, those others and I, and if you aren't careful, one of us will hurt you. I haven't known you long, either, but I don't think I could stand seeing you hurt."

He looked away from me then, as though at a sight only he could see, and then he laughed shortly.

"I don't believe I just warned you against getting involved with me," he said, the amusement apparently real. "If I'd done anything in my life to deserve someone like you—but I haven't, so there's no sense in even mentioning it. Are you enjoying your visit here?"

I nodded, at the same time reflecting that I liked him better without the facade of glib humor. Tall, strong, handsome—he didn't need anything that distracted from those basics. But I needed something, so I smiled shyly at him.

"Louisiana is so different from D.C.," I offered. "Is it anything like where you and the others live?"

"Not my hometown," he responded, looking out again into the dark. "I grew up in Chicago, and a city like that tends to make a unique mark on you. Jeff said something about being from Atlanta, so maybe it's familiar to him. Leslie comes from someplace in California. I don't know all that much about the West Coast, but maybe it's just the same as here. Or maybe she feels as much of a stranger as I do. When you're alone, you can sometimes feel like that even at home."

Once again he was watching something other than the rain-filled night, and in the distance a rumble of thunder rolled through the trees. That seemed to bring him out of his reverie, and he looked at me with another smile.

"I think we'd better go back in before they start to believe we eloped," he said. "In case I don't get to say this later on, thanks for giving me the chance to meet someone like you. I'll never forget."

He touched my hair gently with his free hand, then turned to open the veranda door for me. Stepping back into that air-conditioning was worse with the mist of rain covering me, but I had too much to think about to really notice.

Now that I'd spoken to all three of my companions, I was more confused than ever. At least one of them had been playing games, maybe even two. There was no confusion about that. But, then, why had all three of them lied?

"I CAN UNDERSTAND now why people used to consider conversation an art," Jeff said into the silence that had descended with Brent's and my return. "After no more than a matter of hours, we no longer have anything to talk about."

"We can always try politics or religion," Brent suggested with a grin. "One of those ought to liven things up."

"Mrs. Haines was upset enough about the spilled wine," Jim pointed out from the couch he sat on. "I hate to think what she'd do if we added spilled blood.

I don't know about the rest of you, but I'd dislike being sent to my room and told to stay there."

"Where's your sense of adventure?" Jeff asked while Brent laughed. "And I happen to believe anything can be discussed without the need for spilling blood, even those two topics. But come to think of it, that might not hold true for sports."

"Nonsense," Brent disagreed. "Cubs fans are the most reasonable beings alive. Not only are they cultured and witty, they have the most exquisite taste in ball clubs."

"Absolutely," Jeff assented. "I've heard it said many times that their taste is almost as good as a Braves fan's. Haven't you heard that, Jim?"

"Could be, but I'll tell you what I'd like to hear," Jim said as he looked toward my chair. "I'd like to hear what Carrie thinks. As far as conversation goes, we've all been shortchanging her."

"You know, you're absolutely right," Jeff said as he and Brent also looked at me. "Come on, Carrie, now's your chance. Tell us which ball team you like the best."

Ball teams were the last thing on my mind, but I wasn't so distracted that I began reeling off stats about the Pirates. The real Carrie Tappan might not follow baseball the way I did, so there was only one response possible.

"How about those Mets," I ventured with something of a smile, and all three of them laughed.

"I think that just about says it all," Jeff observed with a chuckle. "The lady would like us to talk about something else, so let's see if we can oblige. How do you find living in D.C., Jim?"

"Crowded, expensive, and hard on the feet," Jim answered with an easy grin. "No one who really likes their car dares to drive through the city, so either you take the Metro or walk. Since I'm something of a snob, I usually end up walking."

"I've never seen the thing, but I understand the Metro isn't all that bad," Brent commented. "The only thing that would bother me is all that underground. If a train doesn't spend at least part of its time elevated, I'd rather have nothing to do with it."

"With what a train ride costs in Atlanta, if you're traveling with someone you might as well take a cab," Jeff noted. "But at least you don't have to worry about being held for ransom. Say, how about a game of cards? Assuming, of course, there's a deck somewhere in this house."

"Now, there's an idea," Brent agreed immediately. "If I don't find something to distract me from these bottles, I'll end up like Leslie. You'll join us, won't you, Carrie?"

"I think I'll go to bed," I told him and the others. "It's been such a long day, and tomorrow we're supposed to hear the will read..."

"And then we'll have another long day flying home," Jim said when I let my excuse trail off. "Getting a good night's sleep will do more for you than playing cards, so you go ahead. We'll struggle along without you."

"At least until breakfast," Jeff said with an encouraging smile. "Sleep tight and don't let the bedbugs bite."

"That's right," Brent agreed. "Pleasant dreams."

I emptied my coffee cup, put it aside, then gave them a final smile before leaving. The smile lasted until I reached the darker dimness of the second floor, then I shared my frown with the shadows. I had some thinking to do before I got cozy with bedbugs, and the first item had to do with paranoia. Was it my imagination, or had all three of them been overly eager to get rid of me?

The faint light from the upstairs parlor let me find my doorknob, and once I was inside my room with my shoes off I sat down to review what I'd learned. Brent, to start at the proper end of the alphabet, probably had nothing to do with the wine-importing business. Aside from the fact that he *hadn't* brought any brandy or cognac—unthinkable for any wine connoisseur *I'd* ever met—he had also used Irish whiskey as a substitute. To top it off he admitted knowing almost nothing about California, the state in which so much of his domestic competition was found. How do you stay in business without knowing what your competition is up to?

And then there was good old Jim. Not only had he said he came from Washington, rather than D.C. or one of the suburbs, he'd also lied when he'd told me about NYU. That was the school where my mother had done a lot of her undergraduate work, and she'd given me a guided tour when I'd considered going there myself. The law school was Vanderbilt Hall, not NYU Law School, and Washington Square Park could be strolled through in about fifteen minutes or less. And maybe people still made speeches in Hyde Park, but there hadn't been much of that even in my mother's day....

Which brought us down to Jeff. I had no doubt that he knew Atlanta, but for a chemist he knew more than most. The difference between Hilton and Vista isn't exactly a topic that comes up most often in everyday conversation. I knew he was supposed to be someone who traveled, but a lot of people who traveled never heard of the connection. And as for that story about why he had no accent...

No, every one of them had been lying, but for what reason? I got out of the chair and paced back and forth, but the pieces refused to fit together. Stopping in the middle of the room, I blew out a breath of annoyance. There had to be two schemers in that house, one possibly after the inheritance.

I took out the pair of light-peach silk pajamas I'd bought as part of Carrie's wardrobe, but not because I intended going to sleep. I got undressed and ready for bed, then pulled out one of the murder mysteries I'd brought with me.

I read for quite a while before tiredness caught up, the muted creakings of the house and the pouring rain doing their part to add to it. Since inspiration was conspicuously absent, I gave up and turned out the light. It felt strange being in a house so big that the comings and goings of others couldn't be heard.

I shivered as I climbed under the covers of the canopied bed, silently cursing that air-conditioning. My thoughts turned shapeless and wordless, and I didn't realize I'd fallen asleep until I was shocked awake by a piercing scream.

Chapter Five

I was out of bed and heading for the door even before I was fully awake. The scream had been fairly close, but not directly outside my room. My nerves were still jangling from the fright the scream had held, which made me open the door cautiously. Turning on a light was out, of course. The last thing I wanted was to outline myself against the darkness of the hall.

And the hall *was* dark. The shadows in the parlor to the right of my room were faintly lighter, but the hall itself, in front of my room and to the left, seemed to hold thick blackness that waited to swallow up whoever and whatever went out into it.

If I hadn't heard the whimpering, I might have closed the door again and let someone else be the fearless investigator. The carpeting under my bare feet was warm and soft, a sharp contrast to the chill of the air and the deep-black darkness. But the person whimpering had to be the one who had screamed, and chances were good that the person was Leslie. She hadn't meant to take knockout drops intended for me, but that didn't change the fact that she had.

I didn't so much step out into the hall as slink around the doorjamb and slide along the wall. If I'd had more of a chance to wake up I might have realized I was jumping in with both feet but without any sort of plan. Whatever had made Leslie scream was out here in the hall with us, and the way my luck was running it could probably see perfectly...and knew exactly what that darker shadow up ahead was.

Then a hand touched my right arm, which meant someone was behind me! Rather than letting me have a heart attack in peace, panic sent my reflexes into instant motion. I grabbed the wrist behind the hand on my arm, moved one sliding step back, then heaved with every ounce of adrenaline-reinforced strength in my body. A muffled yell accompanied the big form thrown over my shoulder, and then the thump of it hitting a carpeted floor.

In the next moment, the man I'd thrown—and it *had* been a man—somehow became tangled up with another unknown. In the pitch darkness I heard a rustle of clothing and the faint thud of contact, grunts of effort, and muffled blows that had to be reaching bodies. Two people were fighting practically at my feet, and I had no idea who they were.

And then one of the two broke loose and ran, his heavy footsteps followed almost immediately by the other's. The shadows raced away toward the other end of the floor, apparently heading for the billiards room. The first shadow flew inside, the second at least three paces behind, and then—

"What the hell is going on up here?" Daniel's voice demanded.

He appeared at the head of the stairs with a powerful flashlight. The stabbing beam blinded me for an instant, and then pure chaos broke loose. Three people came bursting out of rooms on the far side of the hall, and Leslie stood motionless in the pitiless rays of light. Cowering against the wall, a fist jammed into her mouth, her clothes looking as though she'd slept in them....

Which, of course, she had. I moved to her quickly and tried to tell her everything was fine now, but she didn't stop trembling until Brent appeared and took her in his arms. He held her tight while she clung to him, then everyone was there and demanding to know what had happened.

"It was like a nightmare," Leslie quavered, the words spilling from behind the dam of shock. "I woke up with a splitting headache, already in bed but still dressed. I had no idea what had happened to me, so I went looking for someone to ask. I made it to the door, stepped out into the hall, then saw this—this *shadow* between me and that parlor. The shape of the shadow looked funny and—and—then it turned and I knew it saw me. I wasn't supposed to have come out, and it was going to make me sorry I had. All I could do was scream..."

She began shuddering again, and I knew exactly what she meant. There's something terrifying about an unknown attack in the darkness. It makes you forget everything you've ever learned about protecting yourself, leaving nothing but the screaming need to run and run and run...

"And what are *you* doing out here?" Jim said to me, his arm coming quickly around my shoulders. "You're trembling, Carrie, and you're not even wearing shoes. Don't tell me you heard Leslie scream and came out to investigate?"

"She—she wasn't the only one," Leslie said before I could answer. "There was somebody else, and he got into a fight with that shadow thing. Then one of them took off and the other followed. I think they both ran into the billiards room."

I hadn't intended mentioning that, but it was too late to keep it quiet. Everyone exclaimed at once, and Jim's arm tightened around me.

"You poor little thing, no wonder you're frightened," he said with concern. "I think the four of us should have a look in the billiards room, to see if we can't find somebody who enjoys frightening women."

The others—including a grumbling Daniel—immediately agreed, then Leslie and I were being left behind. She looked at me with panic just as I looked at her, and then we were following the four heroes bent on searching for the unknown. Being in the midst of numbers was a lot smarter, just in case the unknown had circled around.

It was the strangest thing, but it took me that long to notice that all four of the men were still dressed. Brent, Jeff, and Jim had taken off their suit jackets and ties, but their other clothes were still the same. Daniel wore jeans and a shirt, and showed no sign of having dressed hastily. Somewhere downstairs a clock bonged twice, then tinkled once. If that meant it was a quarter after two, why was everyone still up and running around?

Daniel slowed as he approached the billiards room, and since he held the light, everyone else followed suit. He stepped up warily and moved the flashlight around, trying to illuminate the whole room at once. Brent made a sound of annoyance and reached to the wall on the left, and three lamps came to life.

"There doesn't seem to be anyone in here," Jeff observed, rubbing his jaw as he looked around. "Are you sure he came this way, Leslie?"

"They," Leslie corrected. "And I'm positive. They ran straight in, so they must still be there."

"I'm sure I heard more than one set of running footsteps," Brent put in. "By the time I came out into the hall, it was all over."

"The same for me," Jim agreed. "If I'd heard a scream I would have been out a lot faster."

"I think we all would have," Jeff said, still looking around. "It's too bad that in this house you have to be right on top of something to hear it. I wonder if there are secret passages in the walls?"

"That does it," Leslie said, putting a shaky hand to her head. "If there are hordes of people running in and out of the walls in this place, I'm leaving. I saw a haunted-house movie when I was a kid, and still have nightmares about it. I need to get out of here."

"The idea of secret passages is silly," Daniel snorted. "I've been all over this house, and if there was anything like that I'd know it. Besides, why use secret passages when the second-floor veranda doors are never locked? If I wanted to sneak in here, I'd climb up and simply walk in. Leaving would just be a matter of walking out again."

Everyone looked toward the doors straight ahead, but no one seemed ready to check the theory. If the mysterious intruders had gone out that way, there was no guarantee they'd gone all the way to the ground.

"This doesn't make any sense," Jim said, sounding fretful. "Why would people break in *here?* Is the map to the stolen treasure supposed to be hidden in something that will soon be taken away? Or are we just getting some real-estate agents eager to be first to list the house?"

"Right," Brent said with a laugh. "But let's not forget which part of the house those treasure hunters were seen in. Maybe they just wanted to get an early date for the prom."

"My dance card's already filled," Leslie told him. "And even if there aren't any secret passages, I'll never get any sleep. Between watching the door and the windows— Daniel, how far is the nearest motel? I'll be ready to go in ten minutes."

"No way, Miss Allyn. I can't take the car out in this rain," Daniel said. "The road we came in on will be a mud sea by now, and we'd be bogged down in nothing flat."

"You mean I'm stuck here?" Leslie demanded, her tone uneven. "I don't believe this. I really don't believe it. . . ."

"Why don't you move closer to Carrie?" Jeff suggested. "The four of us guys can take turns standing outside the doors—"

"And do what if that malignant shadow comes back and hits you over the head?" Leslie wanted to know, running her hand through uncombed hair. She sounded and looked a lot more together, but she was obviously still upset. "Then you would be unconscious or dead, and I'd be left with only Carrie next door to protect me. Thanks a lot, but I'll be better off protecting myself."

She hurried back toward her room, and Daniel grudgingly reached over and flipped a switch on the wall. Feeble light came on along the hallway, enough to let her see where she was going.

"Maybe you'd better leave that on for the rest of the night," Jim suggested quietly. "Whoever it was probably won't be back, but it should make Leslie feel better."

"I was just wondering why it wasn't still on from just a little while ago," Brent said. "I don't remember any of us turning it out after the last hand."

"We didn't," Jeff confirmed. "I remember seeing it when I went to my room. Since you two were already on your way to your own rooms farther down the hall, it couldn't have been one of us."

"It wasn't," Daniel admitted, almost as though he'd done something wrong. "I waited for the card game to break up, and once it did I came up and closed all the lights. I was giving the downstairs a final check when I heard the scream, so I grabbed a flashlight and came back up."

"He could have been waiting on the balcony until then," Brent said, staring musingly at the doors. "Once we were gone and the lights were out, he came in and started prowling."

"They," Jeff reminded him. "Leslie said there were two, which makes this even more bizarre. Did they come together and then argue, or did they arrive separately and trip over each other?"

"If they came together and had a disagreement, they could well be beating each other to pulp even as we speak," Brent said. "What a shame that would be."

"A true pity," Jim agreed with a grin. "Carrie, would you like me to spend the rest of the night in your room? I promise to stay at least five feet away from you at all times, a price I'm willing to pay just to be certain you're all right."

"We could take turns paying that price," Brent suggested, smiling faintly at Jim. "I'd also like to know that Carrie is safe."

"Make that unanimous," Jeff added, his smile even fainter than Brent's. "'All for one,' as the saying goes, as long as that one is Carrie."

"Thank you all, but that's much too silly," I told them quickly in Carrie's shy way. "No one was trying to hurt *me,* after all, and whoever it was is already gone. I don't need company, but I wouldn't mind locking my door."

I looked at Daniel, but he shook his head. "Sorry, Miss Tappan, but it's been a lot of years since anyone last saw any of the bedroom keys. If the locks had been modernized along with adding bathrooms and redoing some of the wiring—but they weren't, and that's that."

"Well, it would have been nice," I said with a shrug. "I'm sure I won't need even that. Good night, everyone."

They echoed the sentiment as I left the room, then went back to talking quietly among themselves. I kept my eyes on the parlor until I reached my room, then turned the light on before going in. Checking behind the door came first, then I tackled the rest of the room.

When I was certain no one had gotten in while I wasn't looking, I took the old-fashioned high-backed chair from near the desk and turned it into a door lock. Jamming the top of the chair under the knob and the back legs into the carpet, I had a barricade that would, at the very least, slow someone down.

The veranda doors had little hook-and-eye catches that were useless against anything but the wind, so I improvised there in another way. The room was still decorated with a number of inexpensive knickknacks that probably weren't worth bequeathing to anyone. I took some of those in pairs, balancing them so they would fall against each other if the door moved. The resulting clatter would be as good as a burglar alarm, giving me enough warning to know I had to defend myself.

I went back to the bed and sat on it with a sigh, trying to figure out just what I was in the middle of. That intruder hadn't been after Leslie, a fact her story verified. That shadow had been heading toward *my* room before she came out and saw it, the only place it *could* be heading at this end of the hall.

Unless it was going to the parlor, looking for that hidden secret Jim had mentioned. I folded my legs in front of me as I considered that possibility, but it just seemed too melodramatic to be true. An attempted kidnapping, a drugged drink and now a secret something strangers were after?

No, the parlor wasn't the answer. The shadow that frightened Leslie was coming to my room, and it had come along the hallway because it hadn't known exactly where I was. Or at least, not which side of the house. It had probably watched the men going into their rooms but had decided against climbing down, going to the other side, then up again. Waiting was a better idea. And then Daniel had come along to turn out the lights....

I didn't quite shiver, but only because part of my mind was wondering about that second shadow. It had obviously reached my door before the first, but it hadn't come in. Had it simply stood still to keep Leslie from noticing it, or was it there for another reason? If there *was* another reason, what could it be?

I moved around until I was under the quilt and then lay back, leaving the light on. I was a very light sleeper when I had to be, assuming I happened to fall asleep. If the choice was left to me, that would not happen.

Just possibly, I should have taken Jim up on his idea of keeping me company. And the others, as well. But would even one of them have kept his word along with his distance? I doubted that, which was why I'd refused...and it wasn't fair that I'd *had* to refuse...damn Miller and his easy assignments...I wanted to go home...but there wasn't anyone to go home *to*...never would be...not for me....

WHEN I FINALLY WOKE up all the way, my watch said it was 9:35 and it was morning. I'd fallen asleep any number of times during the night, but only for catnaps. Any sound at all and I was wide-awake, especially when one of my veranda-door alarms went off.

The small ceramic vase with flowers painted on it had fallen against a ceramic flower basket, bringing me up and out of bed in a heartbeat. Between the thin curtains and the pouring rain I wasn't certain if I saw any shadows. Maybe it was the rain that had shaken the door, or the vase had simply not been balanced properly....

Whatever, I was more than ready to get out of that room. I washed as fast as possible and put on a dress in yellow-tan jersey with long sleeves, then dismantled the rest of my door alarms.

I knocked at Leslie's door on my way to the stairs, but got no answer. Rather than look inside I continued down to the dining room, and found that she'd gotten there ahead of me. A buffet breakfast had been set out for us in warmers, and Leslie was already helping herself.

"'Morning," she said over her shoulder after glancing up to see who had come in. "I can't decide if I'm more hungry or tired, but at least there's something I can do about the hunger. How much sleep did *you* end up getting?"

"Not much," I admitted, walking over to pick up the next empty plate on the stack. "I'm glad we'll be going home today."

"*You're* glad," she snorted. "I'd be happy to get out of here even if I had a houseful of screaming kids to go back to. *That* ought to tell you how I feel about it."

Considering her opinion of children, it certainly did. As for me, I would have been ready to give up all current thoughts of a vacation.

Leslie and I filled our plates with scrambled eggs, bacon, fries, toast and marmalade, then deposited the plunder on the table near two of the place settings. A second trip got us orange juice and coffee—we left the fruit and pancakes and hot cereal for someone else. Or later, considering the way Leslie was eating. She'd taken the chair at the head of the table after collecting all the place cards and throwing them away.

The first of the men to join us was Jim, who sent me a relieved smile before going for his food. I was back in my seat from the night before, which put me to Leslie's left. Jim looked for the place cards, smiled when he didn't find any, then took the seat to my left.

Jeff came in next, with Brent only a moment or two behind, but there were no words over the seating arrangement. The two hadn't quite reached the table when Mrs. Haines appeared, this time wearing a brown dress with white trim. The way she stood said she had something to tell us, which made Jeff and Brent take chairs without comment.

"There was a call earlier this morning from Judge Mansard," Mrs. Haines said when she had everyone's attention. "He'd planned to get here early to read the will, but apparently this storm has already caused severe flooding. Considering that it's still raining, he has no idea when he will get here."

"As soon as I finish eating, I'm calling a cab," Leslie announced, speaking to all of us. "When Judge Whoever finally feels up to doing some reading, he can find me in New Orleans at whichever hotel has the strongest door locks."

"If *he* can't get out here, how do you expect a cab to make it?" Brent asked with a sigh. "It looks like we'll be stuck here longer than we planned."

"And that means we'll have to change our flight reservations," Jeff said from his place to Leslie's right. "Assuming we can figure out when to change them to. Mrs. Haines, does anyone have any idea when the rain will stop?"

"Everyone on the radio seems to have an opinion," the woman answered with a smile meant to be supportive. "No two of them agree, of course, but that's the way it usually is. For myself, I'll be very surprised if it stops before tomorrow at the earliest."

Having given us the good news she turned and walked out, leaving a large pool of silence behind. Leslie had gone back to eating after making her announcement, finishing up the last of her food. Once she was through she put her fork down, finished her coffee, then stood up.

"I'll be in the study, calling a cab," she said stubbornly. "If any of you want to share it with me, you'd better hurry up and pack. I'm all ready to go, and once the cab gets here I'm not waiting for anything or anyone. Think about it, Carrie, and then get ready."

She gave us a firm nod, then was on her way into the study. Our silence continued until she closed the door, and then Jeff let out a breath.

"Obviously last night bothered her even more than we thought," he said. "I'm afraid to think about what will happen when she can't get a cab to come out."

"Or if someone agrees to try, then can't make it," Brent added with a nod. "What are we supposed to do if she throws a fit?"

"Since we can't reach a doctor either, that's a good question," Jim said. "We can start by hoping it doesn't happen, but if it does— Well, maybe it will help if a couple of us show her a lot of interest."

Jim was paying more attention to his food than to the talk, so he may not have seen the way Jeff and Brent looked at him. If "a couple" of them got involved with Leslie, that would leave the odd man out a clear field with me. They didn't like that idea, not when they were fairly certain whom Jim intended to be odd man, but they didn't say so. I would probably consider a comment like that boorish, and they didn't care to have me see them that way.

But that was just the way I did see them, and lack of sleep tends to erode whatever patience I have normally. I suddenly wanted nothing to do with any of them, even if it meant going back to guarding myself in my room. Following Leslie's lead I finished my food and coffee, then got up and headed out of the room.

Protests and questions trailed me, but the men were smart enough not to follow in person. The fact that I hadn't answered or spoken at all must have told them pushing it would not be smart. I left the dining room without an escort and returned to my room.

In the short time I'd been gone, the bed had been made and the bathroom freshened. All my personal possessions were right where I'd left them, including the book I'd been reading. It sat on the small table next to the armchair—

I stopped short as I stared at that book, seeing a piece of paper sticking out of it that looked as though it were being used as a bookmark. The only problem with that was I *had* been using a bookmark, one made of thin, polished copper. The piece of paper was nothing I'd seen before.

My first urge was to rush over and see what it was, but I'm not an amateur. Making sure I was alone in the room was the first order of business, then closing the door for privacy when I was certain I was. Only at that point did I go over and sit in the chair, pick up the book and open it to the place the paper was stuck in.

I'd already read that part of the book, and neither of the two facing pages had any marks on them. I put the book aside after noticing the page numbers, then unfolded the paper. There was writing on the inside that should, by all the rules of secret spy stuff, have referred to a really clever code based on the book. I was all ready for something that ridiculous, but the real message shocked me even more.

"Tommy," it read in a bold, masculine hand. *"Targets should watch their backs and not trust anyone."* It was signed *I. W.B.F.*, with a bunch of flowers sketched in to the left of the signature. There was also

a faint rectangular box drawn around the letters of the signature, looking almost like a card.

A card . . . one that came with flowers . . . "I won't be forgetting." *I. W.B.F.* My mystery man had to be right there in the house!

Chapter Six

It took a couple of long minutes before my mind started working again. Shock doesn't normally hold me still very long, but nothing about that assignment was turning out to be normal. Kidnapping, drugging, terror in the night—and a government agent was in the middle of it all.

"Right next to me," I muttered, looking at the note again. It suddenly occurred to me how inexplicit the thing was, even including the name he'd used. Tommy could be anyone, and would logically indicate that the note was written to a man, and the advice given was no more than two hackneyed statements tacked together. When you use a piece of paper as a bookmark, usually the information on it is unimportant and meaningless.

But he'd expected me to find it fast, to spot something out of place that everyone else would miss. It was nice that he had so much faith in me, but his trust was conspicuously absent. Keeping his identity secret meant he didn't trust me not to betray him, either accidentally or on purpose. He also didn't want to share the reason for his being there, or why the "target" was in danger. Apparently I was good enough to find his note, understand its warning, and protect myself, but not good enough to be allowed to know who he was.

I tucked the note back into the book, stood up and began to pace. It had bothered me when the man had made no effort to meet me face-to-face after I'd saved his life, but now! He and I were both in the same house, and he had to be one of the three men who'd been paying me so much attention. He alone knew I wasn't Carrie Tappan, but that didn't mean he was coming on to Ann Mellion. His role must require that he do the same as the others, so he'd gone at it in a professionally thorough way.

"Damn!" I muttered, feeling foolish and just short of betrayed. He obviously wanted to have nothing to do with me on a personal level, and I felt like an idiot for once believing that he might have. A man from an actual dream would have, but my dream man lived in the real world. He was a big-shot government agent who undoubtedly had a dozen women at any one time, all of them crazy about him and ready to jump at the snap of his fingers.

Or, for all I knew, the man could very well be married!

The more I thought about it, the angrier I got. I folded my arms as I stalked back and forth, looking for more fuel to feed the fire, and suddenly found it. His telling me he was there but not who he was amounted to an incredible professional insult. My poo-poohing the danger last night must have worried him in case I was telling the truth, and he'd had to take the chance of giving me the real scoop. Then he'd let me know who was sending the note, to be certain I wouldn't foolishly dismiss the warning. And to top it all off, he apparently wasn't worried about giving me such confidential information, because he didn't think I was good enough to figure out which one he was!

At another time I might have chuckled and considered whether or not to answer the challenge, but right at that moment I wasn't amused. And the sound of the rain coming down outside was a constant reminder of how we were all temporarily trapped there. With nothing to do in that big, empty house—aside from checking the shadows for prowlers—it would be nice to have something to occupy my time. Like figuring out who the conceited fool was, and telling him off to his face.

The decision made, I left my room before the cautious side of me could protest. Yes, he was an agent of the government, and yes, it was smarter not to mix into official cloak-and dagger stuff, but this went beyond common sense and discreet politics. It was now a personal point of honor to solve the mystery, and that was exactly what I intended to do.

Downstairs, I slowed just a little as I approached the dining room. Bursting in and grilling my three suspects was hardly likely to get me the proper answers, and it would be out of character. What I needed was a plan of attack, preferably subtle, maybe even the unknowing help of others. If Leslie was properly approached...assuming, of course, that she was still here.

When I walked into the dining room, however, all thoughts of planning were temporarily shoved aside. Jim, Jeff and Brent were no longer eating. Brent was crouching and Jeff was down on one knee, both of them wearing serious expressions. Between them was Jim, who lay unmoving on the floor.

"WHAT HAPPENED?" I blurted, drawing their attention as I moved toward them. "Is he—?"

"No, it's all right—he isn't dead," Brent said, standing up with a bleak look. "He seems to be unconscious, but we can't figure out how he got that way. He was heading back to the buffet for more coffee, when he stopped and . . . wavered, I guess you would say. Kind of swayed on his feet for a minute, then zap! Down he went."

"Like someone invisible clouted him over the head," Jeff added helpfully, then also stood. "As far as I can tell he's just out, with nothing else wrong. Is he subject to fainting spells?"

"I have no idea," I answered honestly, staring down at the motionless form. "We only met for the first time yesterday. Will he be all right?"

Both men began assuring me that he would be, but I can't say I was listening. Thoughts about knockout drops were buzzing in my head. Jim, subject to fainting spells? Somehow I didn't think so.

"Where's Leslie?" I interrupted suddenly, wondering about the first victim of the drug. "I noticed that the study door was open on my way down."

"She came out and went straight upstairs," Jeff supplied, brushing my hair back with one hand. "A minute or two later, Jim got up for more coffee. Are you all right?"

"What are we going to do about Jim?" I asked, stepping away from the gentle hand. "We can't just leave him lying there."

"We'll have to carry him to his room," Brent answered with a sigh. "First Leslie and now him. If it gets to be my turn, I'll probably feel relieved. Okay, Carrie. Would you prefer an arm or a leg?"

"You make it sound like we're about to carve him up for dinner," Jeff observed with a faint smile. "Rather than get Carrie in on this, why don't you give me a hand. Sometimes less is more."

"That sounds philosophical as hell," Brent observed back. "Far be it from me to point out what we need right now is the practical. What have you got in mind, O Sage of the Ages?"

"What we're going to do, my practical friend, is get him up on his feet. From there I can shift him into the fireman's carry, just as I learned it at my neighborhood firehouse. Our department was all volunteer."

"You were *useful* at some point in your life?" Brent asked, pretending to be horrified. "Good grief, man, didn't you give any thought at all to the family? Are you out to destroy every tradition we have?"

Jeff didn't answer, but he was clearly amused. A moment later there was no time for amusement, not when they were trying to lift Jim's dead weight. The two men fought and struggled to get him partially upright, and as soon as they did Jeff moved fast. Bending, he maneuvered the unconscious man up on his shoulders, then headed for the stairs.

Brent followed behind Jeff to brace the body on the climb to the second floor, using one hand to wipe the sweat from his brow. I stood in the dining-room doorway for a moment to be sure they were going all the way, then went back into the room.

Jim's saucer and overturned cup lay on the carpeting. I picked up the cup and sniffed it, but the light residue of cream smelled normal. The cup was completely empty, without even a single drop to taste. Leave it to Jim to finish his coffee down to the porcelain shine of the cup, and make sure none of it spilled into the saucer.

I replaced the cup and scanned the room, but looking didn't uncover the answers to any of my questions. I was certain Jim had become the second victim of knockout drops, but who could have slipped him the drug? We'd all shared the same food and drink, and I was the only one who had sat next to him at the table. One of the household staff could have come in after I left, but if they hadn't it was down to Brent and Jeff. Leslie hadn't stopped in after leaving the study.

I straightened up with a sigh, not very happy to have yet another mystery to investigate. I had no idea who was behind this, but a harder question was why. Why feed people knockout drops, then simply let them sleep it off? Of course, if I was the originally intended first victim, I might not have been left just to sleep. But then why would Jim be chosen second?

I headed out of the dining room. An unofficial tour of the house might turn up something useful, and while I was touring I could also be considering. Was I still annoyed enough to want to uncover the identity of my mystery man? If so, what would be the best way to go about it?

I took the back hallway down to the parlor, glanced around the unlit room, then stepped through one of the doors into the ballroom. The huge room had had a giant chandelier suspended from its center, but now the shining crown sat in the middle of the polished wood dance floor looking like a grounded crystal cloud. Dozens of packed barrels littered the room, undoubtedly plunder from other parts of the house.

"Legal looting," I muttered, feeling a strange kind of pain. That house must once have been magnificent, especially during a ball. Glittering crystal, laughing people, an orchestra playing beautifully on the platform to the back... Now its owners were dead and the house was dying, too, but without the dignity that should have been its due. To be pulled apart so that strangers might carry away the pieces...

Feeling like a loathsome scavenger, I left the ballroom to its silent brooding. I crossed the hallway to a door that was supposed to lead to the back of the house and cautiously opened it. Beyond this door was another hallway with seven doors, three to the left, three to the right and one straight ahead of me. There was also a single lamp on the wall, lighting very little. The door directly across the way stood open, so I looked inside it first and found a bathroom. Although clean and relatively modernized, it wasn't quite as nice as the one connected to my bedroom. And it was meant to be used by more than one person.

A quick check of the other six doors showed them opening onto bedrooms, about half the size of the ones upstairs. Three were currently occupied, the other three were not. No personal possessions of any sort lay in the ones on the right side of the hall.

I stopped in the doorway of the last room on the right, the empty room farthest away from the occupied ones. The bed was covered with a dust sheet, and the room looked just as unoccupied as the first two. But the carpeting in front of the closet door appeared darker than the rest, something I hadn't seen in the other rooms.

Walking over to the dark spot and touching it made the cool air feel even colder. The carpeting was wet, as though some dripping piece of clothing had been hung on the closet door for quite some time. Someone who had been out in the downpour had used the room, someone who couldn't hang wet clothing in the bathroom or use the house's dryer... Someone, I thought, who had spent the night there and might still be in the house.

I straightened up and looked around quickly, but no one was sneaking out of the shadows, stalking me in the dimness of the curtained room. It was possible my deductions were totally wrong, that the wet spot was there because someone had removed a stain. But there was a damp smell to the room, caused by the wet carpeting. Surely someone who knew how to remove spots also knew that carpeting didn't dry quickly in that much rain.

If my deduction were true, that meant there was someone in the house who didn't belong there—probably whoever had been creeping around the house last night. But there had been two men who had ended up fighting in the dark. If one of them had used this room, what about the other?

An obvious answer came suddenly, making me feel like a mindless fool. That second man in the hall was my mystery man—who else would have been hanging around to keep an eye on the "target"?

I leaned against the closet door, realizing something else as well. When the two of them had run toward the billiards room, chances were that only one actually ran into it. The second had probably ducked into his own room, only to reappear a moment later with everyone else. With all the excitement going on, the hall lit solely by the beam of a flashlight, who would have noticed him getting his breath back?

That was when I heard the sound, a sound made louder in the surrounding quiet. It was as if a foot had kicked into a door, and it wasn't repeated. An accident, then, somewhere down the hall toward the occupied rooms. It was possible one of the staff had gone back to their room for something, but they would have seen me as they passed the room I stood in, or at least noticed the open door.

I got to the open doorway fast, looked both ways along the hall, then slid out. After closing the door silently, I then moved toward my left, away from the location of the noise. A few feet away was a shadowed opening into a darkened room, a place with shelves that could have been a pantry. I slipped inside, then leaned out a little to look to the right. If someone was sneaking around down there, I'd be able to see them when they passed near the single wall light.

It took a couple of minutes, but I finally glimpsed a form moving out of the shadows down at the other end. That form turned out to be Brent. He was going from one room to the next, quietly checking inside as though searching for someone. But he didn't knock on any of the doors first, and he opened them slowly and quietly, then closed them the same way. Maybe the person he was looking for was supposed to be asleep.

The wet spot in the last bedroom apparently escaped his notice. After no more than a glance inside he came in my direction, but I'd anticipated that and had moved carefully back into the deeper dark. I saw him pause in the open doorway to glance around, and then he was gone. A moment later I heard the sound of a door opening, presumably the door into the kitchen area. When it closed again, the silence returned.

I stood there in the dark for another moment, trying to interpret what I'd just seen. Had Brent been searching for *me*, or had he been looking for his secret accomplice? Or, while I was listing possibilities, was he searching the place in his official capacity as an agent of the government? Any of those choices could be the right one, or it could be because of some point I'd overlooked. The matter was worth spending thought on, but not there in the dark, and not until I'd finished checking around.

I took a step toward the open doorway, a silent step despite the wooden floor. Just as I did I heard a less silent footstep, but it wasn't out in the hall. It was right there in the dark with me, and even as I started running, someone grabbed my arm. I was spun around by a man, then turned again. A big hand clapped itself over my mouth, and an arm went around my waist.

A sound like a muffled laugh came from behind me, a laugh filled with triumph. I'd apparently found the intruder from the night before, but not in the way I'd wanted. . . .

Chapter Seven

The man holding me was strong and obviously larger, intent on holding me captive until he decided what to do with me. Rather than wait to find out what that would be, I brought my right elbow back hard into his ribs. It took three blows before his grip on me loosened, but when it did I was able to pull away.

I was panting when I whirled to face him, and trembling. Slipping out of my shoes took only an instant, and then I kicked at him with the intention of doing real damage. If he closed with me a second time, he wasn't likely to repeat his mistake of underestimating me.

My first kick landed somewhere on his leg, forcing out a curse of pain in response. The second went higher, approximately waist height, then he stumbled past me. Rather than trying to block my kicks or respond somehow, he was heading for the way out. I couldn't be sure, but I thought he might be limping.

The thumping of my heart made it difficult to decide whether to go after him, then it was too late. A door opened and slammed shut, and in the following silence I could no longer hear his shuffling retreat.

NO RISK, NO OBLIGATION TO BUY...NOW OR EVER!

GUARANTEED

PLAY "ROLL A DOUBLE" AND GET AS MANY AS FIVE FREE GIFTS!

HERE'S HOW TO PLAY:

1. Peel off label from front cover. Place it in space provided at right. With a coin, carefully scratch off the silver dice. This makes you eligible to receive two or more free books, and possibly another gift, depending on what is revealed beneath the scratch-off area.
2. Send back this card and you'll receive brand-new Harlequin Intrigue® novels. These books have a cover price of $2.99 each, but they are yours to keep absolutely free.
3. There's no catch. You're under no obligation to buy anything. We charge nothing – ZERO – for your first shipment. And you don't have to make any minimum number of purchases – not even one!
4. The fact is thousands of readers enjoy receiving books by mail from the Harlequin Reader Service®. They like the convenience of home delivery and they love our discount prices!
5. We hope that after receiving your free books you'll want to remain a subscriber. But the choice is yours – to continue or cancel, anytime at all! So why not take us up on our invitation, with no risk of any kind. You'll be glad you did!

After pushing my hair out of my face I groped around until I found my shoes, but didn't put them on again. A two-and-a-half-inch heel can be a really good weapon, especially when it's in your hand.

The door to the right took me back to the outer hallway, across from the dining room. It was deathly quiet and as cold as a mausoleum, a comparison I wasn't quite in the mood to dismiss. I turned right toward the entrance hall and the stairs, not looking forward to walking barefoot on the wooden floor. It would probably be as cold as a block of ice—

"Oh!" I gasped as a big body suddenly appeared in front of me. I'd already stopped short and had begun to raise one of the shoes I held.

Jeff also came to a halt and held up both of his hands. "Don't shoot—I'm unarmed," he said, but the lightness of his words didn't match the worry in his expression. "I didn't mean to frighten you again, but I've been searching all over for— Hey, what's happened? You look like you ran into something serious."

"It was nothing," I answered, trying to get my heart back down where it belonged. "I'm going back to my room, so—"

"Then I'll take you there," he interrupted, still studying me intently. "And don't try to give me an argument. You appear to be two steps away from passing out."

He wasn't far from wrong, but I couldn't find much reassurance in his presence. The shadow who had grabbed me in the pantry *might* have been the intruder from last night, but it could also have been one of the other players in that unbelievable game. The person was definitely male, so that eliminated Leslie,

Mrs. Haines, and the maid, Megin. Daniel wasn't tall enough, Jim was unconscious, and Brent had passed the room in plain sight. That left only my present escort unaccounted for.

"I'm helping, not making a pass, so stop trying to move away from my arm," Jeff said. The words were gentle and serious, but also something of a surprise. I hadn't realized I'd been trying to escape his support.

Wherever Brent had gone, he wasn't in sight upstairs. Jeff walked me down to my room, then began to search it. Behind the door, in the closet, under the bed, in the bathroom, even under the desk and on top of the bed canopy. When he was finally satisfied he went toward the door, but instead of leaving, he closed it from the inside.

"Now you're going to tell me what happened," he said, moving no closer to the armchair I sat in. "I know *something* did, so you might as well give me the details. I'm not leaving here until you do."

"Why?" I asked, studying him. "What makes something that happened to me your business?"

He thought for a moment, then he nodded.

"Technically you're right. It *is* none of my business," he granted. "We've barely known each other long enough to be acquaintances, but that doesn't mean I'm free to shrug off whatever's happening around here. First Leslie ends up unconscious, then Jim. In between we get mysterious visitors in the night, and now *you've* run into something. Can you blame me for wanting to know what that something is?"

"I'm not sure," I muttered, running a hand through my hair. "If I *don't* blame you, maybe I should. Let me think for a minute."

My answer startled him, but he still nodded agreement to my request.

All in all it didn't take very long, but once you look at a problem logically it usually doesn't. As soon as I had the answer I folded my bare feet to my left in the chair, and looked again at my visitor.

"You might as well sit down," I said, gesturing toward the chair I'd used as a door lock. "If we're going to compare notes, this conversation might take a while."

"Compare notes?" he echoed with raised brows, staying right where he was. "I don't understand. I'd like to know what happened to you, but where does comparing come in?"

"It comes in as a consequence of a few minutes' worth of logical thinking," I told him. "Or would you prefer to waste time insisting that you're not my old friend from three months ago? Come on, don't tell me you've forgotten after all."

HE WAS REALLY very good. The blank look he gave me was tinged with confusion, then he let curiosity creep in.

"The most I can get out of what you just said is that you think we've met before," he said at last. "I'll admit I wouldn't mind if it were true, but I'm afraid it's not. *Yesterday* was the first time we met."

"Technically, you're right," I said, taking note of his faint grin and interested expression. "We never *met* before, but we did get involved in a bit of interaction. I'm not guessing, so you might as well give it up."

"Why don't you provide me with a couple of details on what you're not guessing about," he suggested, finally beginning to move toward the chair I'd offered. "I can't very well clear up the misunderstanding without knowing what it involves."

"It involves the fact that you're not who you say you are," I said, watching him carefully. His movement and expression were all casual and natural, with no nervousness, no sense of having been caught. "I have a real thing for doing logic problems in my free time, usually by the bookful."

"Logic problems," he mused, leaning back in the chair. "Is that when you're given a bunch of negative statements, and by eliminating what isn't, you find out what is?"

"That's right," I replied in a singsong voice, then grinned. "Easy as a bakery item that isn't cake, bread, rolls or cookies. Getting that note said you were either Jim, Brent or Jeff. Daniel is too young and too short, and the rest are women. You also aren't the intruder, because I ran into him in the pantry and hurt him. I thought at first you might be, but he was definitely limping, and you're definitely not."

"So I'm your 'it' because I'm not limping," he said, nodding soberly. "I still don't understand how you did it, but you certainly found me out."

"How smoothly we ignore all reference to the note," I said, smiling into that casual, gray-eyed stare. "You thought I'd never be able to separate you from the crowd, but let's see what we know about our note sender. We know he's approximately your build, that he's a consummate professional, and that he knows D.C. well. We also know that he knows *me,* even if the reverse isn't true. Or wasn't true. Are you ready to start eliminating?"

"It's your show," he said, holding both hands up. "Since I'm having more than a little trouble following you, I wouldn't dream of trying to join in."

"How nice of you," I said, continuing to smile. I hoped it was annoying him, or at the very least soon would. "Let's work on the professional part first. Someone in your position has to do his homework. He has to know the people he'll be coming into contact with. Brent called you 'Jeffrey,' the usual name 'Jeff' stands for. You corrected him with your proper name in full, first and middle as well as last. Brent didn't do any homework."

"He could have been pretending not to know," my guest suggested, still considering soberly.

"But there's no reason to pretend something like that," I countered. "If anything, he *should* know his cousin's proper name. He certainly knows enough about me. No, Brent isn't professional about anything but drinking, and he claims not to know D.C."

"But you don't believe him," he said, pointing a finger at me. "You've seen him there dozens of times, so you know he's lying."

"As a matter of fact, I lean more toward believing him," I replied mildly, refusing to get annoyed. "But I don't believe Jim. He calls D.C. 'Washington,' and he has no experience with the Metro. From his comments I don't believe he's ever been on it, and that isn't normal for someone who isn't a bigwig. Taking a cab everywhere will not only break you, you'll miss two out of every three appointments."

"I hadn't realized D.C. traffic was that bad," he said with raised brows. "And I hate to say this, but maybe he never *has* any appointments, or leaves an hour early for them, or has everyone come to him. But of course you'd rather believe he's never used the Metro."

"Whereas *you* have," I said, back to smiling. "You told us how expensive the Atlanta subway system is, then added something like 'but at least it doesn't hold you ransom.' In Atlanta, as in most cities, you pay when you get on. On the Metro, you pay when you get off."

"Possibly you'll remember I also said I travel for my business," he reminded me, now trying to match my smile. "I've visited D.C. a few times, and I've even used the Metro."

"But Atlanta is supposed to be your hometown," I protested, borrowing something of his former bewildered look as I took a chance. "Weren't you supposed to have been born and raised there?"

"So what?" he asked after the briefest hesitation, the look in his gray eyes now hooded.

"Atlanta is a big city," I purred, delighted that my guess had hit pay dirt. "Big cities have this strange habit of *hiring* fire-department personnel, not asking for volunteers. If you learned the fireman's carry at your neighborhood volunteer firehouse, just what neighborhood *was* that?"

His stare had no expression around it. He seemed to be thinking fast and hard, but I wasn't through yet.

"And then there's the part about knowing *me*," I said, widening the smile just a trifle. "For the past ten minutes I've been someone else entirely, but you haven't said word one about it. All that surprise and confusion you showed was for *what* I said, not how I said it. At the very least you should have reacted when I said I fought the intruder in the pantry and hurt him."

"You're using a lot of circumstantial evidence to prove an unprovable point," he said defensively. "Of course I noticed that you're acting differently, but you should see Leslie. Both of you were rattled by the scare last night, and now you say you were attacked in the pantry. I'd probably worry more if you *weren't* affected."

"And I'd start worrying if you gave in gracefully," I countered. "But now that you've mentioned last night again, I have another couple of pieces of circumstantial evidence. Jim's room is the closest to the stairs on this side of the house, and Brent is in the middle on the opposite side. Yours is in the spot mine is, closest to the billiards room."

"So?" he asked, again with brows high.

"One of the two intruders last night was you," I said, trying that smile again. "Brent heard *two* sets of footsteps, and I definitely saw one shadow chasing another after they'd fought. If they'd both gone into the billiards room and out the veranda doors, the second would have caught the first and they would have fought again. Having had experience with the real intruder myself, I know he would have lost."

"But since there were no bodies, you know he didn't," came the reply. "And that's your evidence?"

"My evidence is the fact that he spent the rest of the night in this house," I contradicted. "I found where that was, and it wasn't up here. That means he didn't just slip out of sight, but either climbed down in the rain or waited outside again until the coast was clear. In either case he wasn't pursued, even though the second figure was originally right behind him. That means the second figure broke off the chase."

"And my room is the only place he could have gone?" Jeff asked. "Why couldn't he have doubled back to Jim's room, or even to Brent's? Maybe Brent claimed to hear two sets of footsteps just to throw you off."

"We've already established that Brent isn't professional enough to be our note sender," I reminded him. "And it was the sound of footsteps that brought him out into the hall. Anyone having to go all the way back to Jim's room would have been seen, so that leaves just you. And maybe now's the time I ought to apologize."

"For what?" he asked, a flicker of wariness showing in his eyes. "Mixing me into your flights of imagination?"

"For tossing you over my shoulder last night," I responded, watching him *very* carefully. "You were probably trying to pull me back and away from the intruder, but when I felt your hand on my arm I just reacted. I didn't mean to throw you into a fight you weren't completely prepared for. That you won anyway shows how really unskilled our intruder is."

The flare of indignation was so brief I certainly would have missed it if I hadn't been watching. Telling a man he won a fight through luck rather than skill will really get to him if it isn't true, as it wasn't here. No government agent will survive if he can't take care of himself, and someone else in his place would have muddled the fight badly. The indignant outrage came and went, and then he was in control again.

"I still say you haven't proved anything one way or the other," he maintained. "I'd probably enjoy being this note sender of yours, and the temptation to agree just for the hell of it is there. I just happen to have this thing about pursuing attractive women under false pretenses. I want you to be interested in *me,* not in the man you think I am."

"Oh, but I'm *not* interested in the man I think you are," I told him, suddenly tired of playing the game. He had no intention of admitting the truth, which confirmed the fact that he had no real interest in me. As far as I was concerned, he could stay anonymous for the rest of his life.

"Then why did we just go through all this proof and counterproof?" he asked, this time really confused. "Wasn't there something you wanted to say to the man?"

"All I wanted to say was that I really hate getting flowers," I answered with a shrug. "I've been wanting to say that for some time now, but had no way of doing it. But since you aren't the man I think you are, the message doesn't concern you. Thanks for walking me back to my room, Mr. Allyn."

Those gray eyes showed that it took a moment for him to understand he'd been dismissed, then they showed a definite lack of happiness. Jeffers Wayne Allyn had been given the game by default, and he didn't seem to like that.

"But you still haven't really told me what happened a little while ago," he protested. "How did you end up in the pantry, and in what way were you attacked? And for that matter, how do you know the intruder spent the night in this house?"

"There are a lot of things I know, Mr. Allyn, but you have no claim on any of it," I responded, folding my hands in my lap. "Since you're not the man I think you are, none of it concerns you. Why don't you see if Brent is interested in starting another card game?"

Frustration flashed across his face along with what looked like the urge to argue, but there wasn't anything he could say. He'd already decided against telling the truth, after all.... He wavered for another moment, then stood.

"You may not believe this, Carrie, but I *am* concerned about you," he assured me. "I don't know what sort of detecting you've been doing or what you think you've found out, but poking around can only put you in danger. When you're ready to confide in me I'll be ready to listen, but until then I want your word that you won't go wandering around alone anymore."

"With all the players in this unnamed game, I haven't gone wandering around alone *yet*," I pointed out. "Something tells me that that's a state of affairs destined to continue, so you have nothing to worry about, Mr. Allyn. I expect I'll see you at lunch?"

The way he drew himself up said he hadn't liked my answer. He strode to the door, pulled it open, then turned to glare at me again.

"You're calling this a game, Carrie, but it isn't," he grated. "Whoever's behind what's been happening is deadly serious, and that's why I want you to stay out of it. If you won't back off, will you at least let me know before you do anything on your own?"

I parted my lips to remind him again that he'd denied having any official standing in this mess. The words were half a breath from being spoken, when they were interrupted by a yell. There was a lot of fear in the sound, and this time the voice was definitely a man's.

Chapter Eight

The supposed Jeff Allyn turned immediately and raced out, but I wasn't far behind him. Being barefoot helped me to move fast, so I reached the stairs only a moment after Jeff. The upper hallway was empty, but Brent lay on the polished wood at the bottom of the stairs. As we started down he stirred and looked up.

"Watch out," he croaked in warning. "One of those steps—there's something wrong."

Jeff and I stopped almost on the same breath, then he moved to the left-side handrail while I went to the one on the right. Testing each step before placing any weight on it took us down more slowly, and just below halfway Jeff stopped again.

"There's no step below this section of carpeting," he said, probing at the place with the toe of his shoe. "It looks as solid as the rest, but if you step on it the carpeting gives."

"And throws you off balance," Brent agreed, grunting as he forced himself to sit up. "I was flying through the air so fast I had no chance to grab on to anything."

"There's another section missing on this side," I told him quietly. "One step below the other, but definitely here."

Or, to be more accurate, not there. The carpeting under my toes gave only a little, but it was still enough to cause a serious misstep.

"It seems to be only those two steps," Jeff said as he reached the bottom. "Not that two aren't more than enough. Sit still until I can look you over, Brent."

"No offense, Jeff, but I'd be happier about your looking me over if your field was people medicine," Brent replied, his voice not quite as lighthearted as his words. "Since I'm not a chemical solution— Ouch! That hurts. Is it broken?"

Brent cradled his right arm as Jeff touched it. His face was pale with pain, but he looked relieved when Jeff shook his head.

"It might not even be sprained," he was told. "It's badly bruised and won't stop hurting for a while, but you should be able to use it. Once we get out of here, have it X-rayed just to be on the safe side."

"The way I feel, I'd better have all of me X-rayed," Brent groaned, moving his legs one at a time. "It's pure luck I didn't break *something*, but that's not to say I won't the next time. What in hell is going on around here?"

"Carrie and I were wondering the same thing," Jeff said, hanging his arms on his thighs where he crouched beside Brent. "First Leslie passes out and then Jim, and now you fall down the stairs because somebody booby-trapped them. That doesn't even count what happened last night, even though we're still trying to figure out exactly what that was. I'm almost afraid to think about what might be next."

"Considering the fact that it will probably happen to *you,* I don't blame you a bit," Brent conceded. "Frankly, I'd rather not know anything about it. I'd happily take to my bed and stay there until the rain stops—if I could find some way to be sure the roof won't fall in."

"I think you ought to lie down, anyway, if only until lunch," Jeff advised him. "I'll help you upstairs, and while I'm doing that Carrie can warn Leslie about the missing steps. Do you happen to know if she's still in her room?"

"I have no idea," Brent replied, wincing as Jeff helped him to his feet. "I haven't seen her since she stomped through the dining room. And somebody around here isn't listening. I said I wanted to be the next to be *carried* upstairs. There wasn't a word about limping and groaning."

"When we find out who's doing this, you can lodge a formal complaint," Jeff told him dryly. "In fact, we all can, and I'm beginning to look forward to the time. Walk close to the handrail."

Brent started slowly up the right side of the stairway with Jeff behind him. I hesitated for a long moment, but then went to the left-hand side. I didn't like the idea of being assigned chores by a man who hid behind lies, but Leslie did need to be warned. Brent was lucky that he hadn't been seriously hurt; if there was a second fall, that luck might not hold.

When I got to the second floor, I headed directly for Leslie's room. Her door stood closed, which had to be why she hadn't heard Brent cry out. Or at least I hoped that was the reason. I felt the urge to open the door fast and see, but swallowed it down and knocked instead.

"Don't open that door or I'll shoot!" I heard from the other side, making me very glad I hadn't given in to impulse. "Who is it?"

"Leslie, it's me, Carrie," I answered quickly. "I need to speak to you for a minute."

"Hold on, I'll be right there," I heard, then there was some thumping and scraping. A long moment later the door opened, but not all the way. "I'm not coming out and you're not coming in," she stated. "What do you want?"

"We thought you should know that Brent just fell down the stairs," I said, wondering if she really was holding a gun on me. "He's all right, but it wasn't an accident. Someone removed part of two of the steps."

"Well, *that* was something I needed to hear," she said dryly. "If you happen to run across any ghosts or vampires, don't waste time getting back to me about it."

"Leslie, do you have any idea who's doing all these things?" I asked, trying to keep my voice soothing. "So far no one's gotten seriously hurt, but that could change if it isn't stopped."

"It so happens I do have some ideas, but I'll keep them to myself just now," she said, looking at me with what seemed a lot like suspicion. "If I decide to discuss them, I'll be sure to let you know. Was there anything else?"

"Only that you really ought to consider rejoining the group," I answered with a sigh. "Sitting up here all alone . . . I mean—"

"I'll think about it," she all but growled, then closed the door in my face. Considering the way I'd so gracefully destroyed whatever peace of mind she'd managed, I couldn't blame her. Me and my big mouth.

Walking slowly back toward the stairs I saw Jeff coming out of Brent's room, but he didn't rejoin me immediately. On the way he stopped into Jim's room, and when he reappeared he shrugged.

"Still sleeping like the dead," he reported as he moved toward me, then flinched visibly. "Let's strike that comment. The last thing we need right now is someone dead. We'll hunt up Mrs. Haines and Daniel, and they can do something about the missing steps."

"For how long?" I murmured without really looking at him. "They can be tampered with again as soon as we all turn our backs, or next time the culprits can try something else. Care to make a bet on which way it will go?"

"I'm not feeling that morbid yet," he replied, stopping me at the head of the stairs. "What did Leslie have to say?"

"She was thrilled all to pieces at the prospect of breaking her neck," I answered softly. "That response came after she threatened to shoot me. She's really very unhappy about being stuck here."

"Are you certain she has a gun?" he asked with a frown. His hand had come to my arm again, keeping me from moving toward the right side of the stairs. "That would really be a complication we don't need. A hysteric with claustrophobia waving around a deadly weapon."

"If she flew here, she's probably bluffing," I said. "But that doesn't mean she isn't prepared to brain someone with a chair. Being alone in a room here makes you think of things like that, especially at night."

"If you feel that way about it, I guess I'll have to stay with you tonight," he said, his gray eyes showing amusement despite his attempt at innocence. "After all, I'd hate to be responsible for some poor person getting hit with a chair."

"Guess again," I told him with a faint smile. "Keeping people safe isn't your responsibility. I'll manage just fine on my own."

This time I didn't let him keep me from moving to the right side of the stairs, which meant he had to take the left. With that much space between us our private conversation couldn't be continued, which seemed to bother him. Personally, I thought that being bothered couldn't have happened to a more deserving person.

Once we had gotten down safely, we went looking for the household staff. Going through a door to the right of the stairs took us not into a hall, but directly into the very large kitchen. It was also a very modern kitchen, all chrome and stainless steel with occasional stretches of wood. The giant refrigerator was a built-in side-by-side, and there were acres of counter space, a double oven, and an extra big dishwasher. Old and decrepit can be frightening, but in my opinion nothing beats ultramodern for soullessness.

"I think they're out there," Jeff said, nodding to the right. A murmur of voices was coming through a doorway to what looked like a screened porch beyond. I let him lead the way to the doorway, and once we went through I found I was right. Cushioned porch furniture that had seen better days was occupied by Mrs. Haines, Daniel, and Megin. They seemed to have been watching the rain while chatting.

"You should have rung, Mr. Allyn," Mrs. Haines said as soon as she saw us, immediately getting to her feet. "The staff is small these days, but there's also very little to do."

"That's about to change, at least for a while," Jeff answered, looking at all three of them. "Someone has tampered with two of the steps of the staircase. My cousin Brent has already fallen, and it's nothing but luck that he wasn't seriously hurt. I think Daniel had better do some fast repair work."

All three of them made sounds of shock and surprise, and Megin and Daniel got to their feet. Since Mrs. Haines was already standing, she regained her senses first.

"But that's ridiculous," she protested unsteadily. "What do you mean, 'tampered' with the stairs? And who would do such a thing?"

"If we knew who, we wouldn't have said 'someone,'" Jeff answered. "And you can see what was done by coming to look for yourself."

He led the way back to the entrance hall with Mrs. Haines right behind him, and I brought up the rear behind the other two. Our audience had been skeptical; once they saw what had been done, though, their mood switched to upset.

"Daniel, there should be wood in the toolroom behind the kitchen," Mrs. Haines said, her voice trembling. She sounded frightened. "Get whatever you need to fix this immediately. Megin, didn't you notice the problem when you were up to straighten the guests' rooms?"

"It wasn't like that, Mrs. Haines—I swear it wasn't," the girl answered shakily. "If it was, it would have caught *me* when I came back down. I also cleared the dining room when everyone left, and didn't see anyone near the stairs."

"We already know it was done after that," Jeff said. "After Brent and I took Mr. Nolan upstairs, we came back down again and went looking for Miss Tappan. I happened to find her first, and when I walked her back to her room the stairs were fine. It was a short while after that that Brent fell."

"I don't understand any of this," Mrs. Haines said, putting one hand to her head. "And what did you mean, you and Mr. Lawler 'took' Mr. Nolan to his room? Why did he have to be taken?"

"Apparently Mr. Nolan passed out right after breakfast," Jeff said, watching the woman's hand go to her throat. "Since there's no way to get a doctor here, we simply took him to his room in the hope that he would come out of it by himself, whatever 'it' is."

"The Down luck!" Megin cried, blanching as she clapped a hand over her mouth.

"Megin, don't say that!" Mrs. Haines gasped, turning to look at the girl. "You know very well there's no such thing, and I don't want to hear you mentioning it again!"

"What isn't she supposed to mention, Mrs. Haines?" Jeff asked curiously. "Down luck? What is that?"

"It's nothing but a silly superstition some of the people around here occasionally talk about," the woman answered reluctantly.

"Tell us about it, anyway," Jeff urged gently. "If you like, we'll promise not to believe it."

"You would be really foolish if you did believe it," Mrs. Haines said with sincerity, apparently upset by Jeff's sarcasm. "Talk of it first started over a hundred years ago, when this house was built. Some of the men hired to work on it came down with mysterious sicknesses, or died suddenly. The first work crew quit, and the house had to be finished by a second crew. It was ready only a little past the time it was supposed to be, but the man who had it built didn't move in as planned. He was a wealthy plantation owner named Down, who suddenly wasn't quite as wealthy as he had been. For some reason his business interests had begun to fail, then he and his wife and two sons were killed in a freak accident."

Mrs. Haines sounded hesitant, as though she wasn't enjoying what she was saying. Her face had paled.

"Their infant daughter wasn't killed with the rest of the family," Mrs. Haines continued. "The child was raised by distant relatives, and when she married she came back with her husband to claim the house. They lived here without incident for quite a number of years, but never had the family they'd wanted. Then the woman died unexpectedly, and her husband didn't last much longer. The house passed to relatives of his, but they didn't do any better with it. Some of the stories are so ridiculous I refuse to repeat them, especially since most of what happened had to be coincidence."

"Do you think that's why Aunt Rebecca killed herself?" Jeff asked. "Because she knew it would be her turn as soon as Uncle Desmond was gone, and couldn't bear to wait for it to happen?"

"I don't know," the woman responded in a whisper. "Mrs. Allyn was a wonderful woman who never faced life with fear. If, at the end, she did find something that frightened her, who are we to criticize?"

I think Jeff was about to assure her he wasn't criticizing, but Daniel chose that minute to return.

"Look what I found," he said in disgust, obviously referring to the two pieces of polished wood he carried. Each was about three feet long. "They were standing in a corner of the toolroom, all casual and innocent. I bet anything they'll fit right in as soon as I take up the carpeting. Whoever did this has a hell of a nerve."

"Why don't we get out of your way and let you get on with it," Jeff said. "Come on, Carrie, we can keep each other company in the parlor."

He put out a hand to me, and after the briefest hesitation I joined him. I had the strangest feeling that he wanted to talk to me privately, but didn't care to say so aloud. If it turned out I was right, I had something of my own to say.

When we got to the parlor he closed the door behind us, then moved toward the veranda doors. Opening one of them let us see the steadily falling rain beyond the veranda. Then he turned again and beckoned me.

"Let's stand outside and watch the rain for a while," he said with a smile. "I don't know about you, but I could use a break from this air-conditioning."

I hesitated a second time, but his supposed reason for stepping outside was too close to my own wishes. I needed a little fresh air even if it *was* misty and humid, and even if I did happen to be barefoot. I followed him outside without saying anything, and rather than close the door the way Brent had, he left it open.

"So, what do you think?" he murmured as we stood there watching the gravel of the drive getting ready to float away.

"What do I think about what?" I countered in an equally low voice. "The rain? I adore the rain. Getting trapped in the boondocks by it has always been my private fantasy."

"Someday I'll have to tell you about *my* private fantasy," he returned with a small laugh. "But right now I was talking about the stairs business and that story we were told. Is someone taking advantage of an old legend, and if so, for what reason?"

"However would *I* know?" I asked with exaggerated innocence. "And what difference could the answer to that make to you? When you leave here you'll be going back to Atlanta and the life of a traveling chemist. No one like that has to know the answers to a mystery, so why waste time speculating?"

I kept my gaze on the rain while speaking, as well as during the short silence that followed. His insisting he had no official interest in the goings-on might have seemed like a good idea when he did it, but now he needed to think again. As long as he refused to admit the truth, any theories I came up with were none of his business.

"You're one tough lady," he said at last with a sigh. "Are you sure we can't discuss this like two distant cousins trapped under a common roof?"

"I'm positive" was the only possible answer. "Besides, how could inexperienced little me have noticed three things that didn't quite fit? I couldn't have, so discussions would really be pointless."

Exasperation replaced the amused coaxing I'd heard in his voice a moment earlier. I'd said what I had to get rid of that amusement. If he was allowed to lie, so was I.

"I wonder how satisfying a hobby woman beating would make," he growled softly, then suddenly I was pulled into his arms. "Your attitude leaves me only one choice, so all I can do is go with it."

He lowered his lips to mine so quickly that I had no chance to answer or even to comment. Soft and warm those lips were, determined without being demanding, sensual without being intrusive. The kiss was thorough and totally self-assured, but as soon as I began to struggle it was also over.

"I've been wanting to do that since the first time I saw you," he murmured, then released me with a grin. "Now I can go and consider my choice with a clear head. Don't stay out here alone too long, and remember to relock the door when you do go in."

And then he was gone, striding back into the house and heading for the hall door. He was going to consider his choice, he'd said, but what choice was that? Whether or not to tell me the truth? Whether or not to keep trying for my cooperation? Whether or not to kiss me again?

I turned away from the empty parlor to look at the rain again, fighting to keep my fingertips from touching my lips. I could still feel his kiss there, a kiss I might very well have returned. Somehow I couldn't quite remember if I *had* kissed him back, which was completely ridiculous.

"You're a damned fool," I whispered harshly to myself. "He's someone who won't admit the truth even when he's cornered, so how can you trust him? And don't forget about all those girlfriends. . . ."

I hadn't forgotten the possibility he was taken, either, but somehow I couldn't believe it. There was something honorable about him; if he wasn't free to kiss me, he never would have done it.

So where did that leave me? I leaned back against a door as I tried to figure it out, but no answers came. Was I supposed to tell him I'd enjoyed the kiss, and wouldn't mind if he did it again? But what was the point? Once we left that place I'd never see him again, even if I wanted to. And I did want to, but his job meant too much to him...

The mist from the rain had already begun making me feel damp, but I continued to stand on the veranda for a while anyway. The choice between having an important job and having someone to love...there was no question how I would choose...no question at all...no question and no chance....

Chapter Nine

I was still in the parlor when Megin came in to tell me lunch was ready. I was no more than faintly hungry, so I ran upstairs first for my shoes before heading for the dining room. The stairs looked completely untouched when I used them, but Daniel had obviously done the repairs. I couldn't remember hearing the sound of hammering, though. And hadn't there been something about those pieces of wood he'd found?

Brent was already in the dining room when I got there, checking out the buffet. Just as I joined him Jeff came out of the study, where he paused only a few steps into the room. The reason for his hesitation became clear when Leslie walked in from the hall, but she made a face at us and gestured impatiently.

"You can all stop looking at me like that," she grumbled. "Acting crazy during daylight hours strikes me as being a bit much, so I've decided to save the hysterics for tonight. Where's Jim?"

"Considering your decision, are you sure you want to know?" Brent asked, rubbing his right shoulder. "With everything that's happened lately, hysterics might turn out to be the sanest reaction we can have."

"He means it's Jim's turn to be unconscious," Jeff explained, moving closer to the buffet. "You know, the way you were yesterday. He was on his way to get a second cup of coffee at breakfast when he simply passed out. I'm just guessing that you didn't have all that much to drink, and you don't usually have problems like that."

"I didn't and I don't," Leslie agreed with a frown, looking thoughtful. "The most I had was four glasses of wine, and on occasion I've finished an entire bottle alone without it bothering me. So you think someone *caused* me to pass out, and the same something happened to Jim? What could it be?"

"I think we can eliminate aliens and bill collectors," Brent said over his shoulder. "But everyone else is a suspect. Maybe after lunch we can cross off a few more groups, like one-legged Greeks and brunette beauticians. Isn't anyone else indulging?"

Putting off the discussion until we were seated with our food was a good idea, so I stepped up to the table to see what was there. This time the buffet was cold, with a variety of sandwiches minus all crust, homemade potato salad, macaroni salad, and cole slaw, potato and corn chips with small cups of dip, a plate of pickles cut in quarters, and three different kinds of pop.

A small stack of plates stood ready to hold the sandwiches, and four glasses stood near the pop. Brent helped himself to a little bit of everything, but all I took was a turkey sandwich on a paper napkin and a bottle of Dr. Pepper.

Brent sat at the head of the table, I claimed my usual seat to his left, Jeff took over Jim's place to my left, and Leslie settled on the chair to Brent's right. Jeff and

Leslie had followed my example, which made Brent the only one with a plate, glass, and cutlery. We ate in silence for a short while, then Leslie looked around at us.

"I think it's my turn to ask the questions," she said. "I have my own ideas about who's behind these goings-on, but there's always the chance I'm wrong. What have the rest of you come up with?"

"We can't even find a place to start," Jeff said after glancing at Brent and me. "I'll admit I've been wondering if our inheritances are involved, but none of us know what we're getting. Is it possible someone else does?"

"It's possible, but not very likely," Leslie answered, leaning back in her chair. "On the way here from the airport I tried to pump Daniel, and he all but laughed at me. That Judge Mansard was only a lawyer when he drew up Uncle Desmond's will, but even as busy as he is now he won't let anyone else handle it. He considers it a privileged communication, and no one is going to know what's in that will until it's read."

"So what in heaven's name is going on?" Brent asked, looking around at us with confused eyes. "Why are people breaking in, and other people dropping down unconscious? Or falling down stairs, for that matter? None of it makes any sense."

"Megin thinks it does," I put in suddenly but quietly. "She thinks it's this Down's luck business."

Leslie and Brent immediately began demanding to know what *that* was, but all Jeff did was study me from under half-closed lids. He knew I'd said what I had for a reason, but he hadn't brought up the point himself. If that meant he'd wanted it kept quiet, he should have remembered to mention it to me.

"Jeff was there when Mrs. Haines told us about it," I said, begging off shyly from the demands for details. "He'll be able to repeat it a lot better than I could."

Jeff's glance at me wasn't very friendly, but he had an audience of two waiting to hear the story. He repeated what Mrs. Haines had said without leaving anything out, and when he was through our companions just stared at him.

"They can't be serious," Brent finally said, coming to his senses first. "That's the sort of nonsense they make grade B horror movies out of. Is anyone supposed to take it seriously?"

"Picture yourself being the one to inherit this house," Leslie answered sourly. "If just visiting here has given us such a hard time, what would it be like to move in permanently?"

"I don't care for pictures of that sort," Brent returned, all but washing his hands of the idea. "If I inherit the house, I'll do what I originally intended—sell it so fast the ink on the deed won't be dry yet. Don't tell me any of you intended to keep it?"

He looked around at us, but couldn't find anyone willing to admit they would be that foolish. Of course in my case the decision would be someone else's to make after I claimed the inheritance. Jeff, too, would not be making that decision, not unless he'd been given the real Jeff Allyn's preferences. That half of us could be wiped out without any real heir being affected was almost funny.

"All I know is that I really want out of here," Leslie stated after taking another sip from her bottle of root beer. "If one of us is doing all this to get the heir who inherits to sell, then in my case they've accomplished their aim. Not only am I convinced, but I've even made plans for tonight to stay well out of the path of any more action."

"I think I'm afraid to ask," Brent said with a grin. "For myself I was hoping Carrie would volunteer to hold my hand and put wet cloths to my brow. Considering how that fall has left me feeling, my bedroom is one place she's guaranteed to be safe."

"I'm not surprised, Brent, but my plans don't include hand holding or brow wetting," Leslie responded with a laugh. "I was thinking more along the lines of pit digging and bear-trap setting. Once I have everything in place, I'll give all of you fair warning. If, after that, you happen to get caught, it won't be anyone's fault but your own."

The bright smile she gave Jeff and Brent held smug satisfaction, but that was better than hysterics and threats. And at least she wasn't lumping me in with the others.

"Well, it's back to bed for me," Brent said, pushing his chair back and standing carefully. "I'd invite you along with me now, Carrie, but I've just discovered I'm in no condition for any more social mixing. A pity, really, when it could otherwise have been so much fun...."

As he let the words trail off I could see the strain under his urbane smile, and then he was walking out of the room. He seemed to be in quite a lot of pain.

Once he disappeared into the hall Leslie also stood. "It's time I got back to my bear traps," she said with an easier smile. "I really do appreciate your getting me down here, Carrie. I hadn't realized it was what I needed. I owe you now, but I'll find some way to repay you."

She gave Jeff a nod and then she was gone, striding out with a casual swing to her hips. A moment or two of silence followed her exit, and then Jeff stirred to my left.

"As soon as they've gotten to their rooms, we'll go to yours," he murmured. "There's something we have to talk about."

"We've already used up the topics of sports and the weather," I murmured back. "Since I'm not in the mood to discuss politics or religion, there isn't anything left."

"Stop being so stubborn and at least hear me out."

I looked at him sharply then, but he was glancing casually around the room, as though what he'd said hadn't been very important. It could turn out that he was just trying another line on me, but I was willing to wait and see. If he was, though, he would find himself tossed out into the hall so fast...

He didn't wait more than five minutes, then he stood to hold my chair. I got up and circled the table, but not to lead the way out. I made a stop at the buffet first, and picked up two more bottles of Dr. Pepper that were definitely sealed. The pop would be warm when I got around to drinking it, but I could be sure it would be safe. Jeff hesitated an instant before taking two bottles of cream soda, and then he followed me out.

Brent and Leslie were nowhere to be seen, and when we got to my room Jeff searched it again. As soon as he was certain we were alone, he brought the high-backed chair closer to my armchair and sat.

"Now, then," he said, leaning forward just a little. "You may have noticed I made a telephone call. Would you care to speculate on who I was talking to?"

"Your wife and children?" I suggested, just to see what he would say. Amusement gleamed briefly in his eyes, but he still shook his head.

"I don't have a wife and children," he stated rather than said. "What I do have is a temporary family who adopted me for a purpose, and Dad has given me permission to discuss it. Without his permission, all I could do was keep my mouth shut."

"'Dad' rather than 'Uncle'?" I asked, just to cover the sudden fluster I felt. He could have ignored my comment about his being married.... "And what makes me suddenly good enough to meet your, ah, father?"

"Dad did some checking on you at my suggestion," he replied. "When I called back to say you'd spotted me without my having said a word, he was duly impressed. I was told I could cooperate with you as far as was practical, which means as long as the information exchange is two-way. And yes, he's Dad now and never Uncle."

"Well," I said, trying to figure out the implication of the new arrangement. "So you're now telling me you do have an official interest in what's happened. Since we're supposed to be exchanging and cooperating, why don't you start with the reason you're here. I'm sure you already know why I am."

"I know *now* why you're here," he said, and then he grinned. "But you're saying I have to come across first with some info to prove that my intentions are honest? Is that the way you always handle the men you meet?"

"Standard operating procedure," I agreed with a shrug. "It saves a lot of regrets later on. Besides, I've already given you my analysis of Brent and Jim. That makes it your turn for sure."

"You're right, so let's get to it," he said with a smile. "It all started when one of the agents of the National Security Agency picked up a rumor about the Honorable Russell Tappan. It was one of those whispers that just gives you a name, showing only that someone is talking about the person. Normally nothing would be done beyond establishing a casual surveillance, not until some details turned up."

"But Russell Tappan is in line for an important new post," I said, already beginning to see the picture. "If someone's talking about him, chances are good they intend taking advantage of the situation."

"That's what National Security thought," he confirmed with a nod. "At that point they began to look through his life a little more carefully, and discovered that his only child was due to take an unexpected trip. At home she was practically kept in purdah, but this trip would leave her open and vulnerable. They decided they would feel better having someone along to keep an eye on her. Since I've done this sort of thing for them before, I was elected."

"But you said they knew me and why I was here," I pointed out. "That means they decided to let me play decoy, but without being told the rules of the game. With my eyes closed, I could have walked into anything. Do you and they know what happened at the airport?"

"Yes to both," he answered, and there seemed to be anger in his eyes. "They had some people at the airport just to keep an eye on you when you arrived, and saw that supposed chauffeur make a try at walking away with you. When they reported the incident, they thought it was luck that you happened to break free."

"They sound like real aces," I commented. "Did they get anything out of the man when they picked him up?"

"As you said, they're real aces," he responded with a grimace. "They lost him in the crowds and weren't able to pick up his trail again. With that in view, there's a really good chance he's our intruder from last night. If I hadn't suddenly found myself tossed into a fight with him, I might have been able to keep him from disappearing again."

"He doesn't seem partial to the idea of standing and fighting," I said, trying to ignore the sudden warmth in my cheeks. *I* was the one who'd done that tossing. "If that was him in the pantry earlier, he took off as soon as he saw I wasn't helpless. But that could have turned out worse than it did, also. If they knew I was a professional, why didn't they ask for my cooperation?"

"The current department head has a thing about security and a 'need to know,'" he told me with a head shake. "He doesn't have field experience, so he can't tell where security ends and stupidity begins. They didn't even let *me* know you were the one who was coming here. No sense in warning me and giving me the chance to argue the point."

"Argue the point," I echoed, finding it impossible not to stare at him. "If you'd been given the choice, you would have preferred not having me here?"

"Yes, for two reasons," he said, making no attempt to avoid my gaze. "I've had a bad feeling about this assignment from the minute I walked into this house. It's not going to be easy just because you're a highly competent professional. There's a real chance you'll be seriously hurt, and I don't care to see that."

"And the second reason?" I asked, wishing he would lean back again. Leaning forward had brought those gray eyes too close...*much* too close.

"My second reason is that I wanted us to meet under less official circumstances," he replied, reaching out to touch my cheek with the back of one finger. "I wanted to tell you *my* name, not someone else's, *my* likes and dislikes, *my* opinions and hopes. But I can't, not while I'm working."

At that point he did lean back, but it was no help at all. I wanted him to do those things, too, but you can't ask a man to do something he considers wrong. I could see the problem, but there was something else I couldn't see.

"It's too bad you were so busy during the past three months," I commented, not quite looking at him.

"What do you mean?" he asked, and I glanced up to see him looking puzzled.

"I mean you had three months to drop by," I said, deciding to get it out in the open. "If it was all that important, you would have done it—unless you were just too busy."

"Try changing that to under orders to stay away," he responded, staring straight at me. "That department head I told you about was convinced that my safety during future operations shouldn't be jeopardized by 'hasty disclosures to unauthorized personnel.' I was talked into fighting the decision through channels rather than simply telling everyone where to go. But it wouldn't have been for much longer. I prefer bringing flowers to sending them. That way you find out sooner if the woman hates getting them."

I could feel the second blush more strongly than the first, and this time he noticed and grinned. I was fairly sure he hadn't believed me when I said I hated getting flowers, but that grin was an excellent reason to keep the truth to myself.

"So Dad grounded you for your own good," I said. "I didn't know I was encouraging you to sneak out behind his back, but now he's found out and given you grudging consent. We'll obviously have to keep this strictly business, or he'll throw a fit. Girls from the private sector are never accepted into families with sky-high security clearances."

"I don't mind that you're from the wrong side of the tracks," he said, his grin widening as he reached for my hand. "And I can guarantee I'm not slumming, because I've never done this sort of thing before."

I slid my hand free in a way that I hoped looked casual. "Don't you think we ought to get back to exchanging information? That was supposed to be the purpose of this discussion."

"So it was," he agreed in a murmur, amusement showing in his eyes again. But there was also something else in them...something that said the next time he might *not* agree. "Where did we leave off?"

"You were saying you don't think this assignment is a false alarm, and I agree," I supplied. "That incident at the airport could have been a case of mistaken identity, but the rest of it? I really don't think so. Were you able to confirm the way I did that Leslie was drugged, or were you just guessing?"

"I was guessing," he said with a frown. "How did you confirm it?"

"I got to her wineglass after the three of you carried her out," I told him. "There was a faint residue that suggested knockout drops. But there's something else you don't know. The glass of wine she drank was originally mine."

"The devil you say!" he exclaimed angrily, coming forward in the chair again. "You couldn't have been here more than fifteen or twenty minutes, which means they were prepared in case their try at the airport failed. That's twice in an hour's time."

"And then nothing until the middle of the night," I mused, not having looked at it like that before. "If they were that well prepared, why wasn't something else tried during dinner?"

"Lack of adequate opportunity?" he guessed. "But they had less opportunity in the parlor, and still got to your wineglass. Maybe someone decided they'd be best off waiting. Since the next try was made by an outsider, that would have diverted suspicion from the inside man."

"That's possible, but for some reason it doesn't feel right," I said, shaking my head. "After Jim and I left for our rooms, how long did the rest of you stay?"

"Of the three of us, I left first," he reminded me. "That was about ten minutes or so after you left, and Brent had just poured himself a last half glass of wine. He'd be going up when he finished it, I remember him saying. Translate that to another ten or fifteen minutes, and then Leslie was left alone to pass out."

"Something just doesn't fit," I grumbled, getting up and pacing. "There's always a reason things happen, but this time... Can't Dad come up with something to help, like producing a wiretap? With only one phone in the house, someone could get careless."

"As a matter of fact, there is one," he admitted from behind me. "Four calls were made last night, two of them by you and me. The bad news is, all the calls were garbled. Our equipment isn't getting along with the old-fashioned wiring of this house, and it isn't enjoying all that rain. The only thing we know for sure is that the other calls were made by men. What was said will have to wait until they tease it from the tape—if they can."

"I wonder when the ropes will appear," I said, shaking my head again. "You know, the ones to tie our hands behind our backs while we try to figure this out."

"Don't let it worry you," he said softly from right behind me. "If anyone really tries to tie your hands, they'll have to go through me first. You believe that, don't you?"

I turned to find him no more than a breath away, those gray eyes looking down at me. What he'd said was purely personal, and I did believe it. It might be his job to protect the woman I was pretending to be, but that wasn't at all what he'd meant.

"Believing you is getting easier and easier," I admitted, finding it impossible to look away from him. "I wonder why that is."

"It comes from my dashing profession," he assured me soberly. "One of the department's recruiting points is that this kind of work never fails to impress the girls. But you know, I just thought of something."

"What?" I asked as his arms came up to circle me. I shouldn't have let him do that, but I couldn't seem to move.

"It's occurred to me that we've known each other for three months now, but we've shared only a single kiss." His arms were bringing me closer to him, so close it was becoming difficult to breathe. "A record like that is positively shameful, so we'd better do something about it fast."

And then we were sharing a second kiss, one he began gently but with full self-assurance. It almost seemed as though he were coaxing me after him, teasing me to follow his lead somewhere. My first reaction was that I didn't know him, not really, so why was I letting that happen? The immediate answer was that I *wanted* to know him, and that's all it took.

When I slid my arms around him and spread my hands over his broad back, everything changed at once. It was suddenly a demanding kiss I was responding to, caressing hands that were holding me, a beautifully hard body that welcomed mine against it. We seemed to fit together as though made for each other, as though we'd waited forever for that moment. We tasted each other thoroughly, then he raised his head to smile.

"I think we just made up in quality what we lack in quantity," he said in a murmur. "And I also think it's time I went back to my own room. The best way to ruin something like this is to rush it."

"I suppose you're right," I agreed with something of a smile. "Not to mention the fact that we're both working."

"Yes, I'd almost forgotten that point," he said with a nod as he released me slowly. "We're both supposed to be on the job, and someone around here doesn't like you... Well, I won't be far away, so don't let it worry you. Just keep on defending yourself."

There wasn't much to say beyond that, and no real reason for him to continue to stand where he was. He didn't seem all that eager to go and for some reason I didn't want him to, but we'd agreed it was for the best. His hesitation lasted only another moment, and then he was gone.

It actually took a minute or so to realize I was just standing there, staring at the closed door. I could still feel the kiss we'd shared, the way his hands had stroked my hair and back. I hadn't wanted the time to end, but he'd stopped things by saying he ought to leave.

Ought to. Was it possible he'd wanted me to disagree, but hadn't said so because he didn't care to make me feel cornered? We'd both been waiting a long time to meet face-to-face, and now that we had we both seemed to like what we saw. What if I'd told him I didn't want him to go...?

There was a way to find out. Since I knew where he'd gone, all I had to do was follow and invite him back. I strode to the door and yanked it open, and—

Chapter Ten

And Jeff had suddenly turned into Leslie. She stood outside my door with her hand raised to knock, and was almost as startled by my abrupt appearance as I was at hers. For an instant she tensed, and then she laughed.

"I wasn't expecting to be answered even before I asked, so to speak," she said. "Am I interrupting your going somewhere?"

"No...no, not really," I responded, my cowardly side feeling relieved. What if Jeff *hadn't* been expecting me to disagree with him? "Did you need something?"

"Well, in a way I was looking for company," she admitted, somewhat on the hesitant side. "I've been wanting to take a peek inside Uncle Desmond and Aunt Rebecca's rooms, but at this point I don't feel like doing it alone. If you're as bored as I am, I thought you might like to come along."

I wavered for a moment, as though not quite sure I should, but I really had no choice. If Leslie was coming out of her mood enough to want to go sight-seeing, I couldn't refuse to help.

"I guess I am bored," I lied, wondering if she would notice. "Is there supposed to be something special about the rooms?"

"That's what I want to find out," she replied, stepping back to let me get out into the hall. "Uncle Desmond is supposed to have had a lot of money, but you couldn't tell that by looking at the rest of this house. I'm working on the theory that he used what he had to improve the comfort of his immediate surroundings, and that would mean those rooms. Of course, he could have saved the money and left it to us, but I'll believe that when I see it."

I resisted the urge to shake my head at Leslie's cynicism. What people did with their money was their business; if you spent your life waiting for them to leave it to you, *you* were the one wasting your life. So many people built their hopes around what others would do for them, they never made an attempt to do anything for themselves. Not even when it was possible they could have done more on their own than any help would have given.

"Damn," Leslie muttered, and I looked up to see what was bothering her. We were almost to the doors of the master suite, and coming from the other direction was Jeff.

"Well, are you ladies off on a picnic or something?" he asked pleasantly. "I couldn't help noticing you as I was on my way into my room, and I'm wounded. As the only other conscious and undamaged member of this group, I should have been invited to join you. So what are we doing?"

"*We* are minding our own business," Leslie answered, stepping back from the arm he tried to put around her. "Since you've already offered to do the same, you can do it somewhere else. I don't trust any man in this house, and frankly, having you this close makes me nervous."

"I'm willing to work with that," he answered with a judicious nod, then grinned as he stepped closer to me. "Rather than make you nervous, I'll reserve all closeness for Carrie here. I know *she* doesn't mind."

Leslie wasn't amused by the offered compromise, but her reaction was nothing compared with mine. The arm she'd avoided was now around *me,* and making any sort of a fuss would be out of character. Not to mention the fact that I didn't want to make a fuss.

"Look, we're only going exploring for a little while," Leslie said next with a sigh. "I've had a lot of time to think, and with one thing and another I haven't made any attempt to get to know a cousin I'll probably never see again. I owe Carrie thanks for the help she's been giving, and I owe it to myself to be a little nicer to her. Will it kill you to let us do that alone?"

"Not at all—if you were going to do it over cups of coffee in one of the parlors," Jeff returned. He'd dropped some of the bantering air, but not his determination. "Do you need to be reminded about everything that's been happening in this house? Going exploring isn't the best of ideas, but if you're going, so am I. I have no doubts about you being able to take care of yourself, but Carrie is another story. I'll tag along to keep an eye on *her,* and you two can ignore me if you like. I'll even make an effort not to listen to your girl talk, but you're not leaving me behind."

For an instant I thought Leslie was going to change her mind about the exploring. Her light eyes looked really annoyed despite the lack of expression on the rest of her face, and she stared at Jeff while deciding what to do. I was also being careful about my expression, but not for the same reason. I couldn't decide whether to laugh or be just as annoyed....

Jeff had told Leslie that she could be expected to take care of herself, but I couldn't be. *That* was a laugh if I'd ever heard one, and was obviously just an excuse not to be left behind. Jeff knew a lot better than that, and wasn't the sort to dismiss my abilities simply because I was a woman.

But he also hadn't enjoyed not being part of my previous investigations, and now seemed to be grabbing the first opportunity to take advantage of me through the role I was playing. Carrie Tappan wasn't the sort to put her foot down about his company and send him on his way, especially not with someone like Leslie there. I'd have to go along with whatever she decided even if I didn't agree, and that was just how Jeff wanted it.

Which was a hell of a way to avoid an argument with me. I stirred in the circle of the casual arm around me, wondering if the man ought to be congratulated or stepped on with a sharp heel. I hadn't quite made up my mind when Leslie also stirred, then shook her head.

"I'd love to tell you where to take your ultimatums and what to do with them once you get there. But it's Carrie you're trying to protect, so I guess I can't complain too much. I'd never forgive myself if anything happened while we were together and it turned out to be my fault that she was hurt. If you're there it can be *your* fault, and I'll be off the hook. But you'd better stay out of our way, or all deals are off."

"I'll be as quiet as a mouse," Jeff promised immediately with a grin. "You won't even know I'm there. So where are we going?"

"I've been wanting to take a look around the master suite," she answered with no real hesitation. "Come on, Carrie."

She put a hand in the middle of my back to urge me along with her, incidentally pulling me away from Jeff. He didn't say a word as he let me go, but it gave me the strangest feeling. He wasn't protesting out loud, but some silent part seemed to be unhappy with the deal he'd had to make.

Leslie marched up to the double doors of the master suite, waited a moment, then opened the right-hand one. She stuck her head inside and looked around, then turned to me.

"It's kind of dark in there, so the first thing we want to look for is a light switch," she said. "If it isn't conveniently near this door, my curiosity might wane. Come on."

She edged into the room, opening the door slowly wider, then began groping at the closest wall. The sound of the rain was clearer than in the hall, and that combined with the gloom made me regret having gone along with her. If anyone jumped out at us I'd have to refrain from doing anything for as long as possible, or Leslie would start to wonder about sweet, helpless Carrie. Suddenly I realized how good it felt to have Jeff right there behind me. Because of that, I gave him a silent apology for having thought about stepping on him.

"Ah, here it is!" Leslie said abruptly with satisfaction, and then the click of the light switch brought peace of mind. The gentle glow from two bedside lamps drove away every monster who had been stalking us in the dimness, leaving behind a very interesting sight.

"Well, will you look at that," Leslie said while taking her own advice. "Obviously I was right, and you two are my witnesses. This *is* the place Uncle Desmond spent most of his money. Did you know this was here, Jeff?"

"I had no idea," Jeff answered, sounding as surprised as I felt. "If I had, I would have been in to see it a lot sooner."

I didn't say anything aloud, but I agreed completely. The room we'd entered was magnificent. Crystal vases stood on tables, crystal animals on shelves, crystal glasses in a narrow, built-in sideboard. Even the small amount of light from the lamps created gleaming rainbows everywhere, cool and beautiful yet strangely warming.

Where there wasn't crystal they'd put lace instead. An intricate screen stood to the left, large enough to hide two or three people. Not far from it stood a dressing table covered in blue lace, with a silver-worked set of comb, brush, and mirror on it. Two other small tables had the same blue lace gowns, as delicate as spider webs, as lovely as the silver.

The large canopied bed was right opposite the doors, its curtains partially drawn. The inner curtains were a solid silver lace, and the outer an open-patterned blue. The combination was echoed in the bedspread, and on the drawn curtains on the veranda windows. Everything was delicate and beautiful, and the only touch of another color anywhere was pale rose, in the throw pillows on the bed, the seats of two chairs, and a faint, misty line running through the blue-and-silver carpeting.

"Even if that screen is only silver plated, it's got to be worth a bundle," Leslie said. "Along with the crystal, you can figure two bundles. And if that lace happens to be handmade and imported—hell, that could make it worth two bundles all by itself."

"And since none of this is packed, it goes with the house," Jeff concluded. "The paintings and books and things are ready to be carted off by one or more of us, but this room is meant to stay as it is. I think it's a safe guess that the one getting the house is expected to keep it."

"I wonder what's in there?" Leslie said, looking at the door to the right of the one we'd come through. "Hang on, and I'll take a look."

She walked to the door in the wall to the right, opened it and groped for a light switch. Once she found it she stuck her head in, looked around briefly, then closed the light and shut the door.

"It's a combination bathroom and dressing room," she reported as she came back. "Big modernized bathroom, with a walk-in closet beyond. The light switch turned on the light in the closet, too, but it looked empty. No lace, but a few more crystal pieces."

"Then I wonder what's through that other door," I said, deciding it was time to contribute. The door I meant was in the left-hand wall, painted white like the rest of the room and faintly streaked with blue and silver.

"I guess it's my turn to find out," Jeff said, starting toward the door. "Anybody want to make any guesses before we know for sure?"

"You just hold it right there," Leslie ordered, suddenly sounding angry. "I thought you were going to be so quiet we'd never know you were here."

"Well, I do beg your pardon," Jeff answered stiffly from where he'd stopped only a few feet away. "Maybe it's my imagination, but I think I remember you speaking to me just after we came in here. When you want someone to stay unobtrusive, you usually don't bring them into the group by asking them questions."

"I asked you *a* question, just one," Leslie pointed out, following to stop near him. "It isn't my fault you took that as an invitation to barge right in and take over. If you never learned how to keep your word—"

"*I* never learned!" Jeff replied heatedly. "You—"

Leslie broke in again at that, then the two of them were talking at the same time, each one trying to drown out the other. At first I'd been surprised that Jeff, a professional, would get into a petty argument like that while working. After a moment it dawned on me that that had to be *why* he was arguing. A professional playing a part has to stick to that part, even to the point of foolishness.

So it was Jeff Allyn arguing with his cousin Leslie, not some stranger who made people suspicious by trying to stay unnoticed. The point was clear, but it didn't change the fact that people sometimes say things in anger by mistake. The man calling himself Jeff Allyn was playing a dangerous game, but it might be possible to give him a hand.

Carrie Tappan would never force her way into an argument even to end it, so that course of action was out. What wasn't out, though, was moving quietly around the two combatants toward the contested door.

Neither of them seemed to notice me—hardly surprising under the circumstances—and when I got there I opened it, located the light switch, then looked around.

The room was comfortable rather than elegant, with only a few crystal miniatures arranged on one shelf. One corner held a neat wood desk and chair, with a small two-drawer metal cabinet beside them. The rest of the room was all couches and chairs in matching flower patterns, small tables and lamps, and a sewing machine. The machine wasn't new and looked as though it had been used quite a lot. At the wall opposite the door there was a sideways flight of wooden stairs leading upward, probably to an attic.

There was more light in that room than I'd found in any other room in the house. The ceiling was paneled in large squares, some of which had lit up when I'd flipped the wall switch. There were also floor and table lamps. The curtains on the veranda windows were sheer white, which in better weather would add to the brightness. The colors of the room were beige, tan, white and yellow, all light enough to avoid creating pockets of dimness.

And yet...I looked around the cozy room again, trying to figure out why I hadn't moved more than two steps across the threshold. It was almost as though I'd heard, above the sounds of arguing, a faint creaking that didn't belong with what I saw. The half memory of sound was ominous in a strange way, far beyond the fact that I disliked any room that creaked at me.

"Well, *that* ought to make you happy," I heard Jeff say behind me. "You kept me distracted long enough for your partner in crime to look behind the door we were arguing about."

"Carrie!" Leslie exclaimed. "I didn't see you going over there. What's in the room?"

"A place for sewing and reading, I think," I answered, feeling them come up behind me. "And a way up into the attic, it looks like. It also isn't as cold in here as in the rest of the house."

"If there isn't a door at the top of those stairs, that's probably why," Jeff suggested. "The room has to share its cold air with an entire attic, so there's less of it to go around. Will I be shot at sunrise if I suggest we go up and take a look? I've always loved attics."

"You would," Leslie answered sourly, giving him a glance to match. "Along with dank, gloomy basements, I bet. The perfect spots for monsters and murderers."

"Only monsters and murderers who don't like being comfortable," Jeff countered with laughter in his eyes. "The rest choose rooms like this one. If you're going to be a baby about it, Carrie and I can explore the attic alone."

His arm came around me again at that, but despite his charm-filled version of a leer, I noticed he wasn't taking advantage. The arm around me was warm and friendly, but didn't go any farther than that. No accidental touchings, no suggestive squeezes, nothing that would make me feel cornered or imposed upon. I might not have minded being imposed upon a little, but the man who pretended to be Jeff Allyn didn't seem to want to do it that way.

"You're *not* going to take over running my idea," Leslie told him flatly. "You may have ruined the quiet time I wanted with Carrie, but I won't let you do the same to the rest. I started this, so I get to go first. If you don't like that, you can turn around and leave."

She stalked off toward the attic stairs, leaving Jeff and me to exchange glances. I wasn't the person she thought I was, but that didn't mean the disappointment she'd mentioned was any less genuine. And it *was* Jeff's fault she felt that way, even though he hadn't had much choice. He was there to protect Carrie Tappan. Neither of us felt particularly lighthearted as we followed her, two conspirators put on the spot.

There was a switch on the wall to the left at the foot of the stairs, and Leslie flipped it before starting up. Past her I could see a feeble glow that fit in better with the rest of the house but, aside from that, wasn't terribly appealing. I hesitated at the bottom of the stairs, and Jeff's hand came to my arm.

"What's wrong, Carrie?" he asked softly. "Don't you like attics? If not, just say so. There's no law requiring us to go up there."

I knew Jeff was serious and I really felt tempted, but Leslie stopped where she was to turn and look at me. The outline of attic I could see behind her made me want to shiver despite the probable warmth. I usually had no trouble with places like that, but that particular place...

And yet I couldn't refuse to go. Leslie really wanted to explore that part of the house, but not alone. If I decided not to go Jeff would certainly stay with me, and then Leslie would have to decide between going by herself or giving up on the idea.

"No, it's all right, I do want to go," I answered, giving each of them a brief smile along with the lie. "As long as I don't have to go first or last, that is."

Leslie simply nodded and continued up, but for an instant I had the strangest feeling she was more than simply pleased. I couldn't imagine why she would feel that way, then dismissed the notion. Not liking where I was about to go was obviously making me imagine things.

I started up the stairs without bothering to take a deep breath, but only because I was saving that for once I came down again. Jeff was right behind me, close enough to make me feel slightly better, but not so close that other thoughts distracted me. And then Leslie stopped.

"Now this is what I call an attic," she announced, standing near the top of the stairs and looking around. "It must run almost the whole length of the house, but there isn't much light. There's enough dust to make up for it, though."

She disappeared into the gloom, her movements making the ceiling creak. I followed quickly without thinking about how much I hated that sound, and a moment later was stepping into the gloom myself. No, dark rather than gloom, definitely dark. The light at the head of the stairs was all there was, aside from glimmers of gray coming through what were probably air vents along the walls.

Those small bits of gray, however, showed how big that attic was. Jeff climbed the last stair and stopped beside me.

"Now this is a surprise," he said, peering into the dark the way I was. "There isn't much up here beyond those trunks and things, but at least what is here is neat. My family's attic looked like barbarians came raging through at least two or three times a week."

"If this is what you call neat," Leslie said, "I'd hate to see your definition of dirty. Just look at all this dust. Ugh."

She stopped by one of the four large trunks standing only a few feet away, and put a hand on it. The hand came away coated with what had previously covered the trunk, and she hurriedly wiped it off on the leg of her slacks.

"Just listen to that rain," Jeff said, referring to the thrumming on the roof above our heads. "And it *is* warmer up here than in the rest of the house. What's in the trunk, Leslie?"

"If I can't coax it into opening, we may never know," she answered, crouched in front of the trunk in question. "All of these seem to be locked, but you may have some luck with that one over there. Why don't you try it?"

She'd waved toward a dark, bulky object almost ten feet away, something that might have been another trunk. It stood all alone, wrapped in shadow and silence. I couldn't imagine much that would get *me* to go over there, which was very strange. For someone who used to watch horror movies at night alone as a child, I seemed to be suffering from an unexplained case of nerves. I was as far into that attic as I would go without being dragged, and that decision was firm.

"You don't share on an equal basis, Cousin," Jeff said to Leslie, obviously referring to the way she'd kept the four trunks to herself. "If my trunk opens and yours don't, let's not have any confusion about who gets to look through the contents first."

"All right, all right, first look will be yours," she grumbled. "It's a good thing we weren't kids together, or I'd probably have socked you. Just get on with it."

Jeff grinned at the less-than-graceful way she'd given in, then started for the shape in the dark. My reflexes were generally very good, but that time I outdid myself. He hadn't even finished taking the first step before I yelped and grabbed his arm, stopping him cold.

"What's wrong, Carrie?" he asked at once, his expression asking *me* the same question. "Did you want to come with me? I'm sorry I didn't wait for you, but I just didn't think of it."

"No—no, I don't want to come with you," I stuttered, this time the awkwardness all mine. How do you tell someone you're suddenly afraid of the dark? "I—won't go over there, and I wish you wouldn't, either."

"I see we have a bigger baby than me with us," Leslie said in a very amused way, glancing over her shoulder again. "He'll be less than ten feet away, Carrie. What do you imagine could happen before he was able to get back to save you?"

"I don't know," I admitted, feeling more than a little foolish. And then I got an idea. "I suppose I was just remembering a movie I saw once, in a setting a lot like this attic. A woman found a trunk like these, and she immediately decided she *had* to open it. We were all yelling, 'No, don't do it!' and 'Don't be stupid!' but of course she did. As soon as the lid was up far enough *it* got her, and—and I refuse to think about what it did."

The shudder I gave this time was mostly acting. Jeff quickly hugged me to offer comfort, and Leslie turned her head to look directly at me.

"Now, where could you possibly have seen a movie like *that?*" she demanded, her expression really strange. "I had the feeling you were too gently reared ever to be allowed an experience like that."

"Oh, that movie wasn't *allowed,*" I admitted, fielding the question easily. "It was at finishing school, and one of the girls smuggled it in along with a player. We all had nightmares for weeks, all but the girl responsible. She'd watched so many movies like that, they no longer bothered her. The rest of us also signed up for the basic self-defense course offered—until they dropped it. Too many parents felt that wasn't what proper young ladies should be taught."

"They prefer to have their daughters be helpless if they're attacked?" Jeff asked, cutting into my deliberate babbling. I had been trying to show I was frightened enough to be shaken out of my usual silence, and apparently it had worked.

"I can see where something like that would get to you," Leslie allowed reluctantly, ignoring Jeff's comment. "Frankly, it's beginning to get to me, too, but I hate to back down from nothing but someone's vivid imagination. Maybe we can figure something out that would let us all do what we—"

"Leslie, I have a better idea," Jeff interrupted. "Carrie really doesn't like this, so why don't I make it easier for the both of you. *I'll* be the one to back down, and then it won't be you who makes us leave. And you'll be doing us a favor by not insisting on staying, because we can't leave until you do. How about it?"

She looked at him with what briefly seemed like frustration and anger, but that changed to exasperation as she sighed.

"Oh, all right," she said grudgingly, straightening to brush at her clothes. "I didn't care what was in those stupid trunks, anyway. Let's get out of here."

Rather than waiting for her to reach us, I nudged Jeff into leading the way back downstairs. The last thing I wanted was to leave Jeff where Leslie could challenge him to a quick run into the dark or something. People who are crazy enough to open large trunks in gloomy attics are crazy enough to do anything.

It didn't take long before we were back out in the hall. It was colder there than in the attic, but I still liked it better. Jeff walked along with me, obviously intending to check my room again before leaving me in it. Leslie moved ahead, only to stop at her door to look straight at us.

"Thanks for helping me explore," she said, the words neutral. "At the very least, it broke up the boredom. But tonight, Carrie, you and I have to get together *alone* to talk. We can come to my room after dinner, or something."

She glared at Jeff with that, then disappeared inside her room without waiting for me to answer. I decided I'd probably take her up on her offer just to keep the peace, and led the way to my room. Jeff checked it quickly but thoroughly, then came over to put a hand on my arm.

"What was wrong up there?" he asked softly. "I know it wasn't the memory of some horror movie."

"I'm still not sure," I answered just as softly, very aware of the warmth in the hand that touched me. "For some reason I kept picturing all sorts of monsters hiding in the dark, and was certain you'd end up their lunch if you went to fool with that trunk. That's one of the many benefits in being a girl. You can be as chicken as you like without worrying that it will ruin your macho image."

"I've never believed in being a slave to any image," he responded with a grin, taking his hand back. "I suppose that's what makes me so good at my job. But benefits aside, I'm very glad you're a girl. And I'm also glad I was there with you, even if Leslie didn't like the idea at all."

"She'll get over it," I assured him with a smile. "And I don't think the intrusion was as bad as she wanted you to believe. If it had been, she wouldn't have found so many excuses to talk to you. And *I'm* glad you were there, too."

We stood there smiling at each other, both having spoken about our gladness, but that pretty well covered the subject. After a moment Jeff noticed the silence, and his smile turned rueful.

"Well, I guess it's time for me to be leaving again," he said. "It still isn't a good idea to rush things, so I'll see you later, I guess."

Rather than make me search for something to say to that, he simply turned and left. He'd already closed the door behind himself before I remembered what I'd been thinking the first time, which got me really annoyed. I was an idiot for certain, especially when you considered he hadn't taken any advantage at all in that dark attic. He could have done lots of things in the name of supposedly coming onto my role character, but he hadn't even tried....

That realization made my mind up again, so for the second time I headed for the door. He couldn't have gone far down the hall in that short amount of time, so it wouldn't be hard calling him back. I pulled the door open, and—

Chapter Eleven

And this time it was Jeff instead of Leslie who stood right outside with one hand raised, ready to knock. Again the abruptness of the appearance was startling.

He looked at me like a schoolboy caught in the middle of some mischief.

"I, ah, remembered something I hadn't asked you," he said, groping for an explanation. "Are you going somewhere? If you are, I can come back later."

"No, no, it's all right," I said, the same answer I'd given Leslie. "It wasn't anything important. Come on in."

I stepped back, and he didn't waste a moment entering the room. When I turned to him after closing the door again, he gave me something of a strained smile.

"I, ah, was wondering—I mean, would you mind—can I ask a question?" His conversation was a lot less coherent than it had been, and his gray eyes showed the strangest expression. It was definitely confusing, but at least it let me put off my own chore until I gathered a little more courage.

"A question?" I echoed. "Sure you can, but wasn't that why you came back? To ask a question?"

"Carrie," he said, and the look in his eyes flickered as he called me by a name that wasn't my own. "I know we've really only just met, but... Do you really believe things shouldn't be rushed? I mean, I'm not trying to talk you into something you have no interest in, but I've been thinking about this for three months. Is there any chance...the same thoughts have crossed *your* mind?"

He asked his questions haltingly, as though afraid of what my answer would be. Anyone looking at that situation in a rational way would probably decide we were both crazy, but logic was no longer of interest to me. Maybe we *had* just met, but I was also a believer in quality rather than quantity.

"Have I had the same thoughts for three months?" I asked in turn, beginning to move toward him. "No, not for three months. But two days is another story entirely."

By then I was right in front of him, and he didn't waste an instant gathering me close. His arms were so strong that I felt a thrill run up and down my flesh, a dancing that intensified immediately as our lips met. The hunger I felt for his kiss was something I'd never experienced before. Working or not, in danger or not, I really wanted that man.

This time neither of us hurried the kiss, and it was absolutely marvelous. What ended it was the fact that we were ready to go on to other things, and certain practical considerations had to come first.

"You set the chair under the hall doorknob, and I'll take care of the veranda doors," I murmured in between brief, continuing kisses. "I'd hate to have an interruption we weren't prepared for."

"There better not be *any* kind of interruption," he murmured back. "I've been kept away from you too long already. If someone tries stopping us now, they probably won't survive the attempt."

I chuckled at the way he put that, then we separated to see to our individual jobs. I had no real desire to pile crockery against window doors, but it had to be done so I hurried as fast as possible. When I'd finished the last one and turned away, I discovered I had a surprise waiting. Jeff had closed the curtains around the bed. When he saw my startled expression he grinned.

"Just a little extra insurance," he explained. "If someone manages to get in here in spite of our precautions, they'll still have to open the curtains before they find us. It has nothing whatsoever to do with the fact that I've always wanted to use bed curtains like these. Shut the world out, and shut myself in with a very special woman. What do you think?"

"I think that's the best idea I've heard in a long time," I told him softly with a smile.

He came close to put his arms around me again. I expected another kiss, but he seemed to enjoy doing the unexpected. He bent and lifted me in his arms, then carried me to the bed.

"Something like this has to be done right or not at all," he said, reaching through the curtains to set me down across the bed. He followed immediately to lie beside me, and when the curtains fell shut we were surrounded by dimness. Only the headboard side had been left partially undrawn, and that was enough for us to still see each other.

At least until he began to kiss me again. At that point my eyes insisted on closing, especially when his hand went to my calf and began a slow, caressing rise. His lips and tongue gave me his taste while taking my own; his hand stroked upward to my thigh. All I could do was moan as I pressed myself closer to his strong, hard body. I wanted to touch him everywhere in reach, but his clothes were in the way.

After a little while his shirt was gone, which let me trail my hands over his back and chest. One of his own hands was under my skirt, caressing everything it touched, slowly and lovingly. The other was at the buttons of my dress, taking its time opening them. Despite his comments about having been waiting three months for this moment, he still wasn't about to rush things.

We had to stop kissing to let me slip my dress off, and he took that opportunity to get rid of his pants. After that we were back into each other's arms, and his hands went to my bra. Once it was open and slid from my arms, his lips went to my breasts. He kissed each of them in turn, then began teasing the left one with his tongue. I watched his dark-haired head bent over me for a moment, stroked his hair, then gave myself up to the delight coursing through my body. He still had patience, but mine was rapidly running out.

Somehow we began tasting each others' flesh, and the musky male smell of him made my head spin. When I reached down to encourage his eagerness with my fingertips, he moaned and closed his arms more tightly about me. He was as ready as I was, and that touch seemed to end his patience. He rid us both of the rest of our clothing, then he was crouched over me and beginning to thrust deep inside.

His lips had mine again by the time our bodies merged, and I honestly couldn't remember ever wanting a man more. I met his thrusts and matched them, all the while very much aware of the curtains around us. A secret time it was, two strangers who knew each other in a different world, stealing the time to exchange a love that had taken them by surprise. None of our people would have approved of what we were doing, but the curtains guarded our secret.

I have no idea how long we made love. When it was over we still lay in each other's arms, locked safely away from the world outside. I felt a very great reluctance to change that.

"You know, I've noticed something very strange about you," the man calling himself Jeff Allyn said. He stroked my hair as my cheek rested against his chest, and was apparently in no hurry to get on to other things. "I've come across women more beautiful than you, but none more desirable. I wonder why that is."

"Probably because none of them saved your life," I answered with a faint smile. "That sort of thing produces a great deal of attraction, I'm told, which was why I did it."

"Mmm, I don't know," he said doubtfully, humor in his tone. "Maybe it was the way you threw me around last night. It's always nice to know you're with someone who can protect you."

"Yeah, I'll bet you spend a lot of time worrying over that," I scoffed, raising my head to look at him. "So what do we do now? Pretend this never happened and get on with our jobs?"

"As far as the others are concerned, we do exactly that," he said, the sudden hardness in his eyes visible even in the dimness. "But as for you and me—or at least me— You're not saying *you* want to forget about it?"

"Couldn't even if I wanted to," I admitted, touching his face with one finger. "I really don't believe in rushing things, but this time things are rushing me. How upset are your people likely to be?"

"I refuse to think about that while I still have you in my arms," he replied quietly. "Whatever happens I'll handle it, so don't waste your time worrying. They may think they own me, but I don't happen to agree."

His hand pressed my head back down to his chest, and we lay there for another few minutes without speaking. Holding him while he held me felt so good it was nearly painful, but how much longer was it going to be possible? He'd said his people didn't own him, but when it came to government agencies that wasn't strictly true. The agencies *had* to hold their people close, and most of those people understood and accepted it. If a man couldn't live with that he quit early, but Jeff had been with them for quite a while....

I didn't mention any of that aloud, and even managed to fall asleep for a little while. It felt so good having those arms around me, so safe.... They might not be there long, but while they were I wanted to remember everything about the way they felt. When I awoke, Jeff leaned down to kiss me, then he stirred and stretched.

"I think I'd better get back to my own room now," he said. "It's got to be getting on toward dinnertime, and I don't want to be seen leaving here. You'll have enough to occupy your attention. You don't need to deal with snide remarks, too."

His saying that made me reach over to stop him, and then I pulled his head down for a more proper final kiss. Letting him go meant I had no idea whether he would ever come back, but there was no other choice.

I really hated having the bed curtains opened, but once Jeff had dressed and left I had no interest in closing them again. I repositioned the chair under the doorknob, then went in to take a shower. I was Carrie Tappan again, and she would never be late for dinner.

I chose a semiformal slacks outfit in champagne with matching high-heeled sandals, the only evening outfit I'd brought with long sleeves. The house felt colder every time I noticed it, and the continuing rain didn't help. I removed the knickknacks from in front of the veranda doors, wondering briefly if anyone would take advantage of their absence, then went down to dinner.

Or at least I started down to dinner. I was almost to the stairs, when Jeff and Brent appeared at their doors, so I stopped to wait for them. They were almost to Jim's door, when it suddenly flew open and Jim staggered out to look wildly around. He gave a muffled scream when the other two men approached him out of the dimness, then sagged back against the doorjamb when they stopped short.

"I know you, I think," he said to them, running a hand through his hair. "I don't know what happened, but I think I know you. I woke up a little while ago and couldn't figure out where I was. It's coming back now, but I'm still blurry about details. I hope you know what happened, because I don't."

Jeff and Brent exchanged glances. Jim was all but babbling, and he looked like the warmed-over dead.

"We think you were drugged," Brent told him slowly and clearly. "You're coming out of it now, but you still need a few minutes to pull yourself together. We were heading on down to dinner, but if you like we'll give you a hand."

"No, no, I think I can manage," Jim answered, one hand to the back of his neck. "A quick shower and change of clothes—dinner is almost ready and I'm hungry—I'll shower and come down, and you can tell me—drugged, why drugged?"

He staggered back into his room with that, and the other two waited until he'd closed the door before continuing on to where I stood. Jeff looked thoughtful, and Brent shook his head.

"It almost sounds like he's coming off a bender," Brent observed. "Once he's out of it all the way, he'll probably be ready to kill. I wonder if we'll ever find out who's doing all this."

"I guess you don't believe in the story about Down's luck," I said.

"Carrie, my lovely, I make it a practice never to doubt the supernatural," he answered with a laugh, then took my arm. "But I'd much rather enjoy life and your company, and let others worry about curses from the past. Have I told you how delightful you look tonight? No? Well, then, I'd better hurry up and do it."

He led the way downstairs, positively oozing charm while he chatted, which proved he must be feeling a lot better than earlier. Jeff followed behind us without comment, and I couldn't help wondering what he was thinking.

Leslie waited for us in the dining room with a glass of wine in her hand, and she looked satisfied to the point of smug. She, too, was wearing an evening outfit of slacks and long-sleeved blouse, but hers was blue trimmed with silver. To be honest it was a little on the loud side, but after all the blandness I'd been wearing, even loudness would have made me happier.

We made small talk while waiting for dinner to be brought out, but Jeff addressed most of his questions and attention to Leslie. He seemed really interested in what she had to say, leading me to wonder if he was practicing misdirection or really was interested.

When Megin brought out salads we decided it was time to go to the table, and that's when Jim showed up. His tie looked hastily knotted, but aside from that he was obviously back to normal. After checking the place cards we sorted ourselves out, with Jeff at the head of the table, me to his left, and Leslie to his right, Brent to my left, and Jim to Leslie's right. We all settled in our chairs, and Leslie eyed Jim.

"It's nice to have our fifth back," she remarked. "Are you all the way back, or are your nerves still jittering?"

"My nerves are too well rested to jitter," he returned with a glance in her direction. "After being out to the world since breakfast time, I now feel ready to do the town until dawn. Unfortunately there's no town in reach to be done."

"Well, we can always have another rousing night of playing cards," Brent said with a grin. "Doesn't that make up for the lack of a town in spades?"

We all winced or groaned at the terrible pun, and Jim shook his head.

"Frankly, I'd have more fun spending the night calling some of those 900 numbers," he said. "Even the ones with nothing but recordings on the other end. Oh, excuse me, Carrie. I didn't mean to sound crude, but this—visit—is beginning to get to me."

I nodded to acknowledge his apology, and the other men quickly changed the subject. It was the strangest thing, but something that had been said made me feel it was a clue. I couldn't quite pinpoint the something, but Jeff was also looking thoughtful.

After that we began the meal, and the only unacceptable thing about it was that one of my forks was dirty. It didn't require a fuss being made, so I simply tossed it into the middle of the table and made do with the other fork. The food itself was delicious, and Megin brought me a bottle of Dr. Pepper without being asked.

We were just about to be served dessert, when the lights began to flicker. It was very much like having a wind blow around a candle flame, and we barely had time to begin remarking about it when the lights died altogether. We sat there in the dark for a good couple of minutes, each of us asking "What now?" in a different way. There were no answers immediately forthcoming, but then Mrs. Haines appeared with a real candle.

"Please stay where you are for the moment," she said, shielding the flame with one hand. "Daniel has gone to see what the trouble is, and will have it fixed as quickly as possible. In the meantime, Megin is bringing more of these candles."

"Standing like that, she looks like Down's luck in person," Brent murmured from my left, and he wasn't wrong. The light of the candle glinted off her face to form hills and valleys, making her look like a demented character from a horror movie. It was much too quiet with the air-conditioning silenced, and the still-present cold of the air felt even more out of place.

We waited patiently and, for the most part, without comment, the time interrupted only by Megin's arrival with a candle holder with five candles. She put it on the table just beyond Brent and Jim, then disappeared back toward the kitchen. I was just wishing they'd handed out flashlights instead, when Daniel appeared with one in his hand.

"Well?" Mrs. Haines said, sounding surprised. "Why haven't you turned the lights back on?"

"Don't make it sound like *my* fault," Daniel replied with a scowl. "With that generator we don't have to worry about getting power from an outside source, but now—it looks like someone deliberately wrecked it. Until we can get a repairman out here, I hope you all enjoy living in the dark."

ALL OF US BEGAN talking at once then, or at least most of us. Leslie's expression said she'd been expecting something like that, and her mind had already been made up.

"I knew it!" she said with grim satisfaction. "I knew we should have done something about getting out of here. Now we're trapped, and we'll be lucky if any of us get away alive. I'm calling the police."

"Too bad, but you can't," Daniel said as she stood, impatient superiority on his face. "The phone line is powered by the generator, too. Until the rain stops, we're completely cut off."

"I think the best way for us to handle this is for us all to stay together," Brent announced, obviously trying to calm Leslie. "That way we can keep an eye on one another, and everyone will be all right. If the rain hasn't stopped by tomorrow, one or two of us can try to walk out."

"Leaving the rest of us here to face—whatever it happens to be," she said shrilly with a wild nod. "Sure I'll go along with that—of course I will! In a pig's eye! Carrie, let's go to my room, the way we decided earlier."

Everyone's eyes came to me then, but I had no trouble deciding what to do. I may have half promised earlier to go with her, but doing it at that point would have been stupid.

"I'm sorry, Leslie, but I think Brent's right," I said as gently as I could. "The best thing we can do right now is stay together, and that certainly includes you. Later we can—"

"No, I refuse to trust them," she interrupted, shaking her head. "The only one I can trust is me, so that's who I'll be staying with. You're welcome to come with me, and I wish you would. The rest of you—don't come within twenty feet, or you'll be sorry you did."

She reached over and took a candle from its holder, then stormed out with it. Her storming was on the restrained side in order to keep the flame lit, but the idea was the same. Once again we watched her go, then heads shook and sighs could be heard.

"If this were a horror movie, hers would be the first dead body we found," Brent commented. "If the rest of us are going to stick together, I'd like to recommend where; that upstairs parlor near the girls' rooms. In there we'll be close enough to Leslie to give her a hand if she needs it."

"That's not a bad idea," Jeff agreed, tossing down his napkin and standing. "Why don't we go there right now?"

"But what about dessert and coffee?" Mrs. Haines protested. "The coffee things are already set up in the front parlor, and dessert can be served there, too."

"Business as usual, eh, Mrs. Haines?" Jim said sourly as he stood. "I admire people who can do that no matter what happens, but I'm not one of them. The upstairs parlor sounds better to me, also."

Since we were all obviously in agreement, there was nothing left for the woman to say. She stood uncertainly in place as we passed her on our way to the stairs, her expression impossible to read in the flickering candlelight. Brent carried the holder from the table, and we all followed him. We climbed the stairs in silence, Jeff to my left, Jim to my right, and when we reached the top our flame bearer stopped and turned to us.

"You know, all that talk about dessert has given me an appetite for some," Brent said. "Why don't the rest of you go on ahead, and I'll see if I can pry some loose from Mrs. Haines. If she needs someone to carry the tray upstairs, I intend to volunteer Daniel. My bruises are going to need a lot more healing before *I* do any carrying."

He grinned as he handed Jeff the candle holder, then took one of the remaining candles. We began moving toward the parlor as he headed back downstairs, but only got to go a few feet before Jim took his turn.

"Hold it a minute," he said, talking to Jeff. "If we're going to be spending our time in the parlor, I need to stop in my room first. I've picked up the worst headache in ten states, and if I don't take something for it the first body found will be mine. I'll be right back."

He helped himself to a candle the way the previous two had done, leaving only two candles for Jeff and me. The hall was really dark beyond the small pool of light we carried with us, which was probably what was making me feel so on edge. Something was wrong, and it had nothing to do with the generator being off.

"And then there were two," Jeff murmured as we walked toward the parlor, showing he felt what I did. "If Agatha Christie shows up, we're leaving."

"Why wait for the last minute?" I murmured back. "The word 'leaving' has the ability to brighten up even this mausoleum. If this really were a movie, the homicidal creature would be after me as soon as *you* decided you needed to be elsewhere."

"You can relax, because I'm not going anywhere," he assured me with a grin and a glance. "Wild horses couldn't drag me from your side—unless a mad scientist shows up to hypnotize me. If that happens, all bets are off."

I smacked his arm to show how much I appreciated his sense of humor, but all he did was laugh. He seemed to be in really high spirits for someone trapped in the dark with the bad guys roaming around the shadows. There are people who really do enjoy that sort of thing, but just then I wasn't one of them.

The parlor was dark and gloomy as we entered, too big to be lit from our paltry pair of candles. Jeff headed for a table that stood more or less in the center of the room. He obviously meant to put the candle holder there, but suddenly my uneasiness was increasing. It was as though someone were staring at me out of the shadows, someone who had been patiently waiting.

"Jeff," I began, needing to say something in warning, but it was too late. Just as he put the candle holder down and began to turn, part of one shadow detached itself and hit him with whatever it was holding. Jeff went down without a sound, and the shadow turned toward me.

IF IT HAD BEEN broad daylight and a man dressed all in black had tried to attack me, I would have been wary but fairly self-confident. There in the dark, however, with Jeff lying unconscious on the floor, it was all I could do not to scream.

"Who—who are you?" I quavered, trying to distract the man coming toward me. I was backing away slowly, but couldn't keep it up for long. If I tripped over something unseen...

"Don't run," a heavy whisper answered me, making the chills race up and down my backbone. "If you run or try to fight, it'll go worse for you. Just stand there and you won't be hurt."

The gruff whisper seemed familiar somehow, but not so the body shape of the man. Unless I was completely mistaken, the person who had tried to grab me in the pantry was larger than this man.

And then I heard a footstep behind me, but knew it couldn't be someone on *my* side. The shadow in front of me had to be able to see whoever was behind, but was pretending he didn't. For that reason, when the hand came to my arm I was all set. Just as I'd done the night before with Jeff, I reached for the hand while taking a step backward and sideways. Twist meshed with pull, and the one from behind flew into the one in front.

Both black-clad figures went down, and that was when things really started to happen. Somehow Jeff got back on his feet and headed for them, and the scuffle became a free-for-all dance in the dimness. He got his hands on the bigger of the two shadows, and this time the man wasn't allowed to run. The smaller tried to get his partner loose, but I was there with a kidney punch to discourage that idea. I heard a grunt of pain before the figure whirled on me, and then my left arm was in agony. My shoulder had been hit by whatever the man carried, and I went to my knees with the pain.

There were running footsteps after that, but I couldn't look up until the pain eased to the point of being bearable. The second figure in black was gone, but Jeff had the first one on the floor under his knee. He was in the process of tying the man's wrists with a long, crocheted table doily.

Jeff finished tying the man, then turned his captive to his back and removed the black ski mask. The face was one I recognized: the erstwhile chauffeur from the airport. The man looked wildly around, and Jeff stood up to loom over him.

"Don't even think about trying to make a break for it," he warned the man. "Now that we have you, you won't be getting away again. It's too bad you're the *only* one we have. Now you get to be charged with everything all alone."

"Everything like what?" the man countered with a snort. "Breaking and entering? I can handle that in my sleep."

"I was thinking more along the lines of attempted kidnapping," Jeff drawled in answer, and the man lost his dismissive expression. "He *is* the one you were telling me about from the airport, isn't he, Carrie? And now he's back trying it a second time. The government is really hard on kidnapping, and the only one they'll have to take their anger out on is you."

"Yes, he's the one from the airport," I confirmed as I struggled to my feet. I was trying to support Jeff's attempt to force the man into naming his accomplice, but instead provided a distraction. Jeff glanced at me, then looked again to see that I held my shoulder with my right hand.

"You're hurt!" he said, and hurried over to me.

The man on the floor blurted, "I'm not taking something like *that* alone. We can talk deal—"

And that, apparently, was the signal; the two candles on the table suddenly went out. Jeff shouted, there were running footsteps, a brief scream cut short, and more running footsteps. Jeff had stayed close to me with his arms protectively around me, but nothing came at us. A long moment later there were sounds near the entrance of the parlor, and Brent and Jim appeared. Jim still held a lit candle, but Brent's had apparently gone out.

"What are you two doing in here?" Brent demanded, peering at us where we stood in the dark. "If it's what I think it is, someone should tell you there isn't supposed to be that much noise."

"Jim, relight our candles from yours," Jeff directed, ignoring Brent. "I think what we've just been doing is wasting our time."

I had a good idea what Jeff meant, and as soon as Jim relit our candles the guess was confirmed. The man we'd caught, who had been about to name his accomplice, lay unmoving on the floor, the hilt of a knife sticking out of his chest.

Chapter Twelve

"This is totally insane," Jim kept repeating, looking really shaken. "What do you mean, someone is after Carrie? Why would they be? And how did it come to this?"

"Someone was in here waiting," Jeff answered. "When I put the candles down they tried to knock me out. I was able to shift with the blow, but it stunned me for a moment. I heard the first person tell Carrie not to run, that she wouldn't be hurt, then saw the second come up behind her. By then I was on my feet again, so I launched myself at the two of them. The first got away, but I caught the second. He was about to tell me who his friend was when the lights went out."

"Courtesy, no doubt, of the first, who hadn't gone far," Brent summed up, also looking upset. "That's one way of making sure no one spills the beans, but for my taste it's a bit extreme. What do we do now?"

"That's a really good question," Jeff said. "With the phone out, there isn't much we *can* do. Carrie, are you sure you're all right?"

"I'm pretty sure nothing's broken," I tried to soothe his anxious stare, giving him a smile. "I'm going to be bruised for a while, but that's all."

"That's enough," he muttered with a savage look. "When I get my hands on him..."

He let the words trail off, but the sentiment was still very much with him. It made me feel strange to have a man who knew me act protective, but it was a nice strange. Most everyone else had always assumed I could take care of myself.

What sounded like a stampede came from the hallway, lots of footsteps and a good number of voices. We all looked at one another, trying to figure out what was going on, but the answer was quickly supplied. A group of men in raincoats led by Daniel entered, and one of them stepped ahead of the others.

"Police," he announced, glancing around at us, then at the body. "What's going on here?"

Everyone tried to answer at once, of course, making the next few minutes pure confusion. It helped that the police had brought flashlights with them, so it was eventually possible to sort everyone out. Jim and Brent were taken out into the hall to be questioned, and Jeff and I were left with the chief deputy in charge and an older, but official-looking, man.

"I'm Harlan Mansard," he said, introducing himself to us. He was still tall and straight despite his gray hair, and spoke with a lovely Southern drawl. "I expected to meet all of you when I read Desmond's will, not in the middle of the night over a dead body. What's been going on here?"

"That's what *I'd* like to know," the chief deputy, named Keller according to his name tag, put in. He was a burly man with a florid face, but his dark eyes looked calm and competent. "When Judge Mansard here called me, we thought someone was playing a joke on him."

"I received an anonymous telephone call telling me something strange was going on out here," the judge supplied. "I also thought it was a bad joke, but when I tried phoning here to check on it, I discovered the line was out of order. That was when I called the sheriff's office and asked if they had vehicles capable of getting through."

"You certainly made good time," Jeff remarked, once again looking thoughtful. "The phone couldn't have been out for more than fifteen or twenty minutes before you got here."

"Nonsense, young man," Judge Mansard corrected. "The phone was out almost two hours ago. It took us all this time to get out here, which is purely a shame. A few minutes earlier, and that man would still be alive."

"And then we'd also have his friend," Keller said, apparently having understood there was another culprit at large. "Why don't you tell me what happened from the beginning."

Jeff went over the story again, for the second time covering up the contributions I'd been forced to make. While he spoke, I spent some time thinking about what we'd been told. The phone's being put out of commission more than an hour before the generator was tampered with didn't make any sense. After all, why waste time accomplishing something that your next effort will take care of? Could the generator have been an afterthought, something not originally intended?

Well, whatever it was, tampering with the phone had gotten us help. Jeff's people had had the line tapped, and they must have known at once when the phone was disabled. If it hadn't been them making that anonymous call to the judge, there was no one else it could have been.

"And then the candles went out," Jeff was saying. "The second one must still have been in the room, and heard that he was about to be named. He silenced his friend here in the dark, then got away before Jim and Brent showed up. I know he's still in the house."

"I'll have some of my men take a good look around," Keller said, rubbing the back of his neck with one big hand. "Don't know that they'll find anything, though. Too many places to hide in old houses like these."

"Maybe I can help you out with that," Jeff said slowly. "I've been doing a lot of thinking about what's been going on, and I believe I've found some answers. Would you be willing to bring everyone in the house together and give me the chance to prove it?"

"Like in a Charlie Chan movie?" the deputy asked with a snort. "Things don't work like that, Mr. Allyn, not in the real world. Why don't you—"

"Please, Deputy Keller," I interrupted, having finally come to a few conclusions myself. "This is a lot more complex than it looks, and we can probably save you a good deal of time investigating dead ends. I don't know which part Jeff has figured out, but I also have something to contribute."

"You two are ganging up on me," he accused, but heavy curiosity lurked in his eyes. "All right, all right. I'm a fool for going along with this, but we'll give it a try. How about in here?"

"I think we'd be better off in the dining room," I countered at once. "The presence of a dead body makes even the innocent nervous."

"Good point," Keller agreed when Jeff nodded. "Okay, the dining room it is. But while you're talking, I'll still set my men to searching."

Jeff and I had no objection to that, so Keller went off to give the necessary orders. Judge Mansard gazed at us speculatively but didn't say anything. Jeff took my hand briefly to squeeze it, but I wasn't sure if that made me feel reassured. Our jobs were almost over, but where would he and I be left afterward?

It took a while to get everyone down to the dining room, and that included Leslie. At first she refused to open her door, and once she understood there were police in the house, she began demanding that they take her back to New Orleans. It was an effort getting her quieted down, but eventually we were all present and accounted for. Judge Mansard, Jim, Brent, Leslie, Mrs. Haines, Daniel and Megin all sat at the table that hadn't yet been cleared. The police stood around and behind us, and Jeff and I stood beside Keller.

"Ladies and gentlemen, we have a dead body upstairs," Keller announced into the silence. "Someone in this house is responsible for the body, and I'd like to know who that is. Mr. Allyn and Ms. Tappan think they can help me find out, so I'm temporarily yielding the floor to them. Please give them whatever cooperation they need."

"I'll go first," I said before Jeff spoke. "My contribution should make Jeff's part easier to understand. The way I see it, our intruders had their plans all made, but someone else came along with plans and did a job on theirs. Both Leslie and Jim were drugged, Brent fell down the stairs, the phone line was cut, then the generator was wrecked. I'm willing to bet that the only thing the intruders were responsible for is the generator."

"But that doesn't make any sense," Brent protested. "If *they* weren't responsible, who else could it be? And why?"

"Why is just as obvious as who, if you look at things properly," I answered. "Why did four out of five of us gather here? To hear a will read. Was there an estate about to be divided up? Sure, among those of us here. If any of us inherited the house, would we have kept it after everything that happened? Or would we have sold it as fast as possible, even if we had to sell cheap?"

"After hearing about Down's luck?" Brent asked with a shudder. "I've become a firm believer, and if I happen to be the unlucky one..."

"It's funny you should mention that," I said as he let the words trail off. "Down's luck. Judge Mansard, you've lived in this area for a while, and you also knew the Allyns for many years. Have you ever heard of Down's luck in connection with this house, or any adverse story at all?"

"Certainly not," the judge answered with dignified outrage. "I'm sure there are places with unsavory or unnatural reputations, but this house isn't one of them. If there were any stories about, I'd certainly have heard."

"But that can't be true!" Megin protested in confusion. "I know there's a story about Down's luck, because I heard it from—"

"Yes?" Judge Mansard prompted when the girl cut herself off short. "You heard it from whom?"

"She heard it from Mrs. Haines, just as the rest of us did," I supplied when Megin simply looked trapped. "I'm sure she was told not to mention it, but she blurted it out as soon as she heard about Brent's fall. Just as she was expected to, right Mrs. Haines?"

"Why ask me?" the woman returned, sweet confusion dominating her. "I've had nothing to do with the goings-on in this house."

"It might be possible to prove that you did, once the bottle of knockout drops is found," I disagreed. "Even if there aren't any fingerprints on it, the police should be able to trace it back to the person who bought it. And then there's the matter of the missing pieces of steps."

"What about them?" she asked, finally looking a bit disturbed. "Do you expect to find fingerprints on them as well?"

"I expect to find that those pieces are *made* to come out," I said, and watched her pale. "The ends of them were too even and weathered to be freshly cut. If I had to guess, I'd say they were part of an old burglar trap, meant to catch anyone in the house who shouldn't be there. How long have you lived and worked in this house again? The only one who knows it as well as you do is Daniel—"

"He had nothing to do with it!" she blurted, sitting straighter as her son stared at her openmouthed. I'd been hoping that suggesting Daniel might be guilty would get her to talk. "He had no idea about how I felt. I've lived and worked in this house most of my adult life, and I'm the only one who loves it the way Mrs. Allyn did. With her gone it should belong to *me* now, not one of a pack of useless vultures! With the money I have saved I could have bought it for a reasonable price, but none of you would have *been* reasonable. That's why I took steps to make sure that you were."

"By playing games with knockout drops," I said with a nod. "You coated one of the glasses set out for Brent's wine, leaving to chance which of us drank from it. Repeating the stunt at dinner last night would have been too obvious, so you saved it for breakfast this morning. I wondered why Jim had been made a victim, when he was supposed to be nothing more than an observer. Then I remembered that Leslie had thrown away those place cards you'd set up so carefully. He took the seat that was meant for Jeff or Brent, and the drug was probably on his spoon. When he stirred his coffee with it, he drugged himself."

Her stare was stony and silent, but the look in her eyes confirmed what I'd said.

"And tonight you tried for me," I couldn't help adding. "But the coating on my fork made it look dirty, so I didn't use it. That was bad luck, but you'd already arranged to add to everyone's unhappiness. Those coffee things you mentioned that had already been set up—set up to get more than one of us, I suspect. And most of us used the phone last night, so you expected at least one of us to do so tonight. That would have been when we found out it was out of service, and you were hoping Leslie would be joined in her hysterics."

"And instead it brought help," Judge Mansard said with a lowering frown. "That's what I call poetic justice. There will be charges filed in this matter, Deputy Keller. Mr. Lawler could have been seriously injured when he fell, and any of the others could have had a violent reaction to the drug."

"I'll be sure to see to that, Judge," Keller answered while Mrs. Haines simply closed her eyes. "But right now I still have a dead body needing explaining, and that has to come first."

"Then maybe I'd better take *my* turn," Jeff said, sending me a glance filled with approval. "Carrie's explanation does make things clearer, and also confirms my thinking."

"Then get right to it, Mr. Allyn," Keller offered, and Jeff stepped forward with a smile.

"My pleasure," he said, looking around at everyone. "Someone I recently met pointed out how useful logic is when you have a mystery to solve, so I've been trying it. It's led me to a few interesting conclusions, but first let's go over what's been happening."

He got a few narrow-eyed looks at that, as if to say we all knew what had been happening. I didn't join in, of course, even though I had a better idea than everyone else. Almost everyone else.

"Stripped to the bare bones, the events have been as follows," Jeff said. "When Carrie arrived in New Orleans, an attempt was made at the airport to kidnap her. The attempt failed, so the guilty party tried again last night and a third time this morning. The man was big, and undoubtedly relied on his size to intimidate. When it came to fighting he knew almost nothing, so each of his three tries came to the same nothing. That's why there were two attackers earlier tonight—an extra effort made to finally get somewhere. The big man was the one I caught, and the other was his secret superior, already in this house."

There was a good bit of stirring and glancing around at that, but no one said anything. Everyone also looked guilty, but that was standard for the situation.

"Now comes the part where we start eliminating people," Jeff went on. "There are four men in this house—me, Jim, Brent and Daniel. I'm out because I was seen fighting with the man, and Daniel is out because he's too small. Jim and Brent showed up after all the excitement was over, but neither of them was dressed in black. They wouldn't have had the time to change clothes, even if they had put the black clothes on over their regular ones. Since that lets them out, who are we left with?"

"No one," Brent blurted, appearing confused. "You've just eliminated everyone in the house."

"Not quite," Jeff disagreed, while the others murmured comments. "I'd been thinking the same, but let's view it from another angle. We all know for certain there were two intruders in the house, but what if there were three? Could the third have helped cover up the tracks of the second, the one who was running everything? He certainly could have, so let's see if we can figure out who *he* is."

This time everyone looked stunned, but I couldn't help feeling very satisfied. I'd thought *I* might have to mention the third man, but Jeff hadn't missed him. He was so beautifully bright, the man calling himself Jeff Allyn.

"Now, the ringleader knew there would be men in this house, and he didn't want Carrie getting involved with the wrong one," Jeff resumed. "He wanted her available for the kidnapping, with no innocent bystander around who might spoil things. For that reason he provided a man to be close to her, one who would try to monopolize her attention to the exclusion of everyone else. He would also be handy to explain away any unsuccessful tries as mere cases of coincidence—or mistaken identity."

"Now, just a minute," Jim huffed even as he paled. "I don't know if you realize what you're saying, so let me tell you it happens to be actionable. You have no solid proof to accuse me, and I insist you withdraw the slander immediately."

"Maybe *I* can help him out," I said before Jeff could reply. "At the airport, you left me alone while you went to get our luggage. When our late friend lost me and I made my way back to where I'd been, I ran directly into you. You said you'd returned because the bags hadn't yet come down, but when we went together to get them, most of those on our flight had already claimed theirs. That means the bags *had* come down, so you had to be there for another reason. What other reason than to make sure the kidnapping had come off the way it was supposed to?"

"And then there's the matter of your origins," Jeff added, putting on the pressure. "Carrie said you came from her family lawyer's office, but I'll bet they don't really know you there. I bet that if the police do some digging, they'll find you don't qualify for being in the job you have. You certainly haven't been in D.C. long, and I'm sure *that* can be proved as well."

"I want a lawyer," Jim grated, now so pale he looked about to pass out. I hadn't told Jeff anything about Jim's association with the Evans law firm, so he must have gotten it as background data. He'd tried a stab in the dark, and it had hit dead on target.

"That's very wise of you," Jeff said with a nod. "When Brent suggested we all congregate in the upstairs parlor, I was surprised at how quickly and solidly you backed his suggestion. It was your job to do that, I think, a job given you by the dead man upstairs while you were getting dressed. If Brent hadn't made the suggestion, you would have."

"Because they were waiting for Ms. Tappan up there," Keller said, his first words in a while. It was clear he wasn't having any trouble believing Jeff, and clear as well to an almost-trembling Jim.

"You're not saying *I'm* the one who's the secret leader in this thing, are you?" Brent nearly squeaked, all traces of cynical humor gone. "I give you my word I had nothing to do with this, and you yourself said I *couldn't* be the one. Come on, Jeff—!"

"No, you're not the one," Jeff interrupted, and relief made Brent the next one to look as though he were about to faint. "The ringleader was well away from the parlor by the time you and Jim got there, just as he planned to be."

Now Daniel appeared nervous, but then he remembered he'd also been eliminated. That left everyone feeling more confused than worried, most especially Keller.

"You've done it again," he pointed out to Jeff. "You just eliminated everyone in this house, so what now? Or isn't the ringleader really someone who was a guest here?"

"Oh, he's a guest, all right, and I do mean 'he,'" Jeff responded. "And I didn't eliminate *everyone,* since the others are four women. But we can do some eliminating in that direction, too. Carrie is out because she was there during the fight, and Mrs. Haines is out because she really is Daniel's mother. Megin's outfits leave no doubt, so who are we left with now?"

"You have a hell of a lot of nerve," Leslie said to him as everyone's head turned toward her in shock.

"As soon as I can get to my lawyer, I'm going to sue the hell out of you."

"What are you going to sue me for?" Jeff asked with very faint amusement. "For saying you're not a woman, or for saying you're the ringleader? Everything points to both conclusions, so which one do you want to tackle first?"

"I don't know what you've been smoking, but you'd better give it up," Leslie answered, leaning back in her chair. "You're dead wrong, and there's nothing you can say to prove that nonsense."

"Sure there is," Jeff countered. "When you were the first victim of the knockout drops, it really threw me off. Carrie and I thought the drug had been meant for *her,* and that you took it by mistake. We now know how that worked, but the aftermath also helped to confuse us."

This time no one said anything, but a vague disturbance was beginning in Leslie's eyes.

"When you came out of the drug, you screamed the house down," Jeff went on. "You saw a shadow figure that terrified you, one that had even started toward you to silence you. When the figure ran, you even told us in which direction. Since that was the dead man upstairs, I couldn't understand what your game was.

"And then I saw Jim's reactions when *he* came out of the drug. He was terrified of Brent and me, even though he knew us. He was also very confused and was babbling, saying the first thing that came into his head. Had had no idea what had been happening, and he admitted that as well.

"And that was when I knew you had accidentally wrecked your own plan," Jeff said, his smile increasing. "When your partner realized that *you* were the one screaming, he must have started toward you to find out what was wrong. He knew where your room was, after all, but he didn't know you'd been fed a drug. You must have been absolutely furious when you were finally back to yourself, but still saw how you could take advantage of what had happened."

"By trying to get out of here as fast as possible?" Leslie asked, sarcasm thick in her voice. "Yes, that's a plan worthy of the best of masterminds. I'm sure they all run away with their tasks uncompleted."

"But you *didn't* go," Jeff pointed out. "I'm sure you really did try to get a cab, and if you had you would have insisted that Carrie go with you. Then you would have had her all to yourself, probably in a place you'd already prepared. When no one would come out, you decided to play the terrified woman whose strange actions would be completely overlooked. The first thing you tried was that exploration of the master suite I invited myself to. If I hadn't, you would have had Carrie all to yourself."

"All to myself in a couple of dangerous rooms," she said with a snort. "Yes, that *would* have been awful for her. Fighting off the lace in the bedroom or the flower patterns in the sewing room. Not to mention having to cope with my conversation. You must be proud of having saved her from that."

"That wasn't all those rooms contained," Jeff said, not in the least bothered by her sarcasm. "I wondered why you insisted on going in first everywhere, but the answer's obvious. You had your pet intruder hiding in the suite, but only you and Carrie were supposed to be coming in. When I barged in, you had to give the man time to hide. You did that, but didn't know *where* he was hiding. That's the real reason you spoke to me when we'd agreed you'd ignore me."

"Right," Leslie agreed with a sober nod. "I didn't know where someone was hiding, so I spoke to you. Did I think you knew where the hiding place was, and if I got you talking you'd tell me?"

"You were trying to let your friend know exactly who was with you, and that he'd better stay out of sight for a while," Jeff answered. "Talking to me told him all of that, and also explains why it bothered you when Carrie looked in the sewing room first. You'd checked the bathroom and he wasn't there, so that left only the sewing room, you thought—until you caught sight of the attic stairs. Then it was obvious where he'd gone."

"And that's where the creaking I'd heard came from," I said triumphantly, finally understanding why I'd been so nervous. "No wonder I felt there was something in the dark of the attic that was up to no good."

"He was waiting for Leslie to maneuver me to where I'd be in easy reach," Jeff said with a nod. "That supposed trunk she directed me to—he probably showed her where he was when she first went up the stairs, then hid. If you hadn't stopped me, I would have walked right into his hands."

"As a mastermind, I don't seem to have done very well," Leslie said, apparent amusement on her face. "Most masterminds would have given up at that point, to save themselves embarrassment."

"You weren't sent here to give up," Jeff pointed out with no trace of humor. "You tried again to get Carrie to go with you after dinner, but wrecking the generator also wrecked that possibility. Even so, you didn't give up. When you marched out of the dining room tonight, you made sure to tell Carrie that she was the only one you would allow into your room. Just in case your next plan didn't work, you wanted to have a backup ready."

"And her next plan was the ambush!" Brent declared, pleased with himself for having seen that. "The dead man wrecked the generator, and she marched out all alone. She probably ran up the stairs to get to her room, where she put on black over her clothes. Then into the parlor, to wait where her other accomplice would direct everyone. When I decided to go back down looking for dessert, I played right into her hands. Jim told me he'd gone back to his room for some aspirin, which got *him* out of the way. That left only you to guard Carrie."

"And I think I just figured out where the intruder went after he missed me in the pantry this morning," I put in. "When the coast was clear he went to *your* room, Leslie. That's why you refused to let me in when I came to tell you about the stairs. He was right there, and I might have seen him even if he'd hidden in the bathroom."

"This is all pure nonsense," she scoffed, waving one long-fingered hand. "Either you're all on drugs, or you're all crazy. Whichever it is, I don't really care. All I want is out of here."

"I'm sure you do," Jeff drawled. "But if you think I've forgotten the other half of my accusation, you're wrong. When we found you passed out from the knockout drops, Brent and I started to carry you upstairs. We had such a hard time of it, Jim had to come over to help us. He clearly didn't want to, but if we'd continued struggling like that we might have touched something we shouldn't have. He helped us in order to keep your secret."

"And he definitely wasn't happy about it," I added. "He'd already brushed off your pretended come-on to him, even though it was probably intended to let the two of you talk. When he helped Jeff and Brent carry you, he was very careful about where he put his hands. Obviously he didn't like the idea of touching any more of you than he absolutely had to. He must have a thing about cross-dressing, even when it's done for a purpose."

"His attempts to be gallant also didn't work very well," Jeff said as Leslie all but glared at a sullen Jim. "There are a lot of examples, the latest being at dinner tonight. He mentioned calling 900 numbers, then apologized to Carrie for any offense she might have taken. You were also at the table, but he ignored you. Even when you were nearly in hysterics after coming out of the drug, it was Brent who calmed you. Jim didn't so much as pat your shoulder."

"All of which means absolutely nothing," Leslie said, getting to her feet. "You have no proof, so you can't stop me from leaving here. I—"

"Ah, but proof isn't hard to get," Jeff purred. "In fact, you can easily prove me a liar. The police are right here, so why don't you show them part of one breast. Having to do that can help your case against me, so why not give it a shot? You're not going to claim you're too shy, are you?"

"You don't have to be shy to refuse to strip in front of a roomful of men," Leslie snapped, reddening. "The police use matrons for women prisoners, and they didn't bring any."

"You're absolutely right," Jeff said quickly, the look in his eyes bright. "It would be unreasonable to ask you to strip in front of all these men, so we'll appoint Carrie the job of matron. You can turn your back to the rest of us and prove your womanhood to her alone. That will settle the question once and for all, and in the most reasonable way possible."

Only then did Leslie understand he was trapped. Jeff had suggested the outrageous knowing he would refuse, then had pounced with the utterly reasonable. To refuse now would be as good as admitting his guilt. Leslie's face twisted and he made a run for it, but the police weren't asleep. There was a brief tussle, and Leslie's shirt was "accidentally" torn open before it was over. The hairy chest underneath the padded bra said it all, and he was dragged back in handcuffs to stand in front of deputy Keller.

"And I thought I'd never see the day I couldn't tell man from woman," Keller muttered, looking at Leslie's real, shoulder-length hair. "I never would have tumbled to this one, not in a million years. We can start the rest of the investigation by trying to find out what happened to the real Leslie Allyn."

"I want a lawyer!" Jim repeated shrilly as the deputies began to cuff him as well. "I had no idea he was going to kill someone, or I never would have gotten involved!"

"Shut up!" Leslie snarled, his furious face still looking like a woman's. "If you tell them anything, you'll regret it! I still have—"

"That's enough," Keller interrupted. "Read both of them their rights, then put them in separate cars. That just about wraps it up, except for searching the house. Most of what we're looking for should be in the—lady's—room."

"The clothes and mask should be, unless he threw them out a window," Jeff agreed. "He had no way of knowing the police would be here, and when he found out he might have panicked. He'd still intended trying to get Carrie to his room later, and might have saved the clothes to wear when taking her out of the house. Since he'd gotten rid of all suggestion that he was a woman before going into the parlor, he had every reason to believe his disguise was still good."

"But none of that says why they wanted *you,* young lady," Keller said, the curiosity back in his eyes. "You're a very pretty girl, but I don't think that explains it."

"I would say that finding out who my father is will answer your questions," I replied with a faint smile. "You might be best off contacting one of the federal agencies about this. Your two prisoners undoubtedly belong to a group, and I have a feeling the agencies will want details on it."

Keller's brows went up as he nodded, then he went off to see about wrapping things up. Jeff and I stood alone for the moment, so I smiled at him.

"It's too bad you couldn't say that you *knew* two men had used the phones along with us last night," I murmured. "Jim couldn't have been one of them, or he never would have mentioned 900 numbers. You need touch tone for those numbers, and all that's here is rotary."

"I also couldn't mention that Leslie probably came back for more wine after that call," he responded, his voice just as low. "If your glass was the one that had been drugged, Leslie would have gone out before Brent left him. He probably came back, took a fresh glass and hit the jackpot. But I feel really stupid for not having twigged sooner."

"Not as stupid as I feel about Jim," I said. "After what William Evans did to him, I should have known there was something wrong."

"What did he do?" Jeff asked. "He sent him with you, so I was considering that Evans was in on this."

"But Evans didn't trust Jim," I pointed out. "Originally my traveling companion was supposed to know the truth about me, but at the last minute Evans decided against it. If James Nolan really was the erring son of money and position finally coming back to the fold, Evans would have let him share the secret. He must have had no choice about sending him, but refused to do it any way but blind."

"Maybe he noticed that Nolan wasn't raised to money and social position, just the way I did," Jeff suggested. "He wasn't even very familiar with what's considered ordinary manners. He had no idea that ladies were supposed to be served first, or that in these circles a gentleman stands when a lady joins him at table. If he'd been raised in a wealthy family he would have learned that, even if he later decided not to do it. He wasn't refusing to do it—he simply didn't know that he should."

I nodded and was about to add something, when Judge Mansard came over. He had Brent with him, and he smiled around at us.

"Now that the excitement is over, I'm going to take advantage of being here," he said. "There's no reason not to read the will right now, then you three can head home as soon as the rain stops."

Judge Mansard thought that was a very good idea, but the rest of us glanced at one another. We were finally going to learn who got what, even if some of us no longer wanted to.

Chapter Thirteen

"But what about the real Leslie?" Brent asked, still looking shaken. "I can't believe— You don't think they did something terrible to her? She and I have never met, but she's still family."

"The authorities will find out, and until then we can only pray," the judge told him with a hand to his shoulder. "Come on now, and let's get this over with. With more than half the heirs in attendance, there's no reason to delay."

He borrowed two flashlights from the police, then led the way to the front parlor. Jeff and I had exchanged glances, but certainly hadn't said anything. There was only one real heir in attendance, which was amusing in a warped way.

When we were all settled in chairs, the judge produced the will from inside his raincoat. He went through the preliminaries quickly, then reached the part that concerned us.

"'To my nephew, Brent Lawler, I leave the contents of my wine cellar,'" the judge read. "'If he has anything of my sister in him, he'll sell his inheritance and use the money to set himself up in a decent business. If all he has in him is his father, he'll drink his inheritance and set himself up with a permanent hangover. In this the choice will be entirely his, along with all credit or blame. Think about it before choosing, Nephew, since this is probably your last chance.'"

Brent looked embarrassed, but he also looked thoughtful. Obviously Desmond Allyn had been keeping tabs on his relatives, and knew what Brent's situation was. It was clear Brent *would* consider his choices, but from his expression the decision would be a battle.

"'To my nephew Jeffers Wayne Allyn,'" the judge continued. "'I leave the contents of my library, which is carefully cataloged. Your father always despised the written word as a waste of time, but your degree and profession suggest you overcame so low an influence. In view of this, I direct your attention to my collection of first editions. May they give you as much pleasure as they gave me.'"

Jeff looked surprised and very pleased, which was, of course, the proper reaction. The real Jeff Allyn had to be in protective custody to keep him from suddenly showing up and compromising his stand-in. I wondered how pleased *he* would be, then dropped the question as the reading continued.

"'To my niece, Leslie Allyn, goes the furniture from the upstairs parlor,'" Judge Mansard read, hurrying through. "'With all that furniture to clean and polish, you should be in absolute heaven. Et cetera, et cetera, more of the same. Ah, here we are. 'To my wife's niece, Carrie Tappan.'"

His gaze flickered to me with a smile, then he was reading again.

"'To my wife's niece, Carrie Tappan, I leave the pieces of artwork listed below. These aren't the best pieces, but they're worth enough to give you a nice nest egg. If you would like to use the proceeds from their sale to make a whole life for yourself, please go ahead and sell them. Living under someone else's thumb can be unbearable, but without life skills escape is impossible. Use the money until you've learned enough to support yourself, but above all try to be happy.'"

I couldn't look at anything but my hands just then, but not because I thought it was the proper response. Carrie had known nothing about her aunt and uncle, but they'd obviously known about her as well as the others. They'd given her a way out of the trap, but would she be able to take it? And even beyond that, would it be safe for her to take it? If she'd been the one in my place the past couple of days, would she have made it through?

"And that's it," Judge Mansard said, beginning to refold the will. "Inventories have been made for all of your bequests, and complete lists will be supplied you. Shipping arrangements can be made through my office or, if you prefer, the items can be put up for sale. There are still papers for you all to sign, but that can be done through the mail. And now—"

"Just a minute," Brent said, a frown creasing his brow. "We heard what all the bequests are, but nothing was mentioned about the house and the rest of its contents. Don't tell me it goes to the state to pay back taxes or something."

"No, not at all," the judge answered with an odd, twisted smile. "Despite Desmond's illness, the Allyns had enough cash to pay all their bills. The rest of the estate was left to another heir entirely, someone you'll never guess."

"Mrs. Haines," Jeff and I said together. The idea was ludicrous, and because of that fit in perfectly with everything else that had happened.

"Exactly," the judge confirmed in surprise, stopping Brent short in the middle of ridiculing laughter. "You two really are good, aren't you? If that woman had just waited for the reading, she would have understood that *she* was the only real family Desmond and Rebecca had. They knew the woman's husband had deserted her years ago, and they didn't want her thrown out of the house that had become her home. I doubt if she's repentant over having been caught, but once she learns the truth... Well, that's for the future."

He got up then and left to see how the deputy was doing, and the rest of us followed along. There wasn't anything left to be said, not with all the mysteries finally solved.

Some of the deputy's men were still searching the house, and two of them were working on the generator. They'd radioed back to their office for people from the coroner's office, and the parts needed for the generator—and the phone—would be sent out with them. It would be a while before all the police were gone, but the judge was able to get a ride with those units carrying Leslie, Jim and Mrs. Haines. We all bid the old gentleman good-night, and once he had left Brent turned to Jeff and me with a wry smile.

"I think my flashlight and I will be going upstairs now," he said. "We have some thinking to do that's waited too long already, and I'm sure you two would rather be alone. I hate to admit it, but you do make an attractive couple. Just don't do anything I wouldn't."

He gave Jeff a wink as he patted my arm, then he was heading out of the dining room and toward the stairs. Keller was using the dining room as his command post, and people kept hurrying in and out of the dark.

"So much for no one noticing there's anything between us," Jeff muttered as he looked around. "I'm sorry, Carrie."

"What makes Brent's nosiness your fault?" I said. "And he might be doing nothing more than guessing, so don't worry about it. As long as I don't start attacking men in the middle of the entrance hall, Carrie's reputation should come out just fine."

"It's not *her* reputation I was thinking about," he responded, gray eyes bright in the glow from candles and flashlights. "I believe it's time I went to my room, but first I'll get a couple of candles and walk you to yours. Being alone won't be possible anywhere in this house for a while, so we'll be better off being apart. You agree, don't you?"

"Oh... sure," I said, reluctantly telling myself he was right. I kept wanting him to take me in his arms, and if we stayed together I might end up saying so out loud. Separating was a much better idea—at least until all the police were gone.

Jeff got two candles and walked me to my room, then did a quick check before he would let me go in. In the instant of privacy we had before he left he kissed me, quickly but with feeling and promise. If the police cleared out before daylight came...

I went to the bed and lay down with my clothes still on, thinking about that wordless promise. It made me forget about the rain that continued to fall, the stuffiness growing with the air-conditioning off, the sound of men calling to one another in the hall. I just wanted the promise to hurry up and be kept, hurry up and become a reality.

I didn't know when I feel asleep, but when I awoke the first thing I noticed was the cold. The generator had obviously been fixed. Then I noticed the daylight. The entire night was gone, which probably meant the police were, too. If Jeff hadn't come to wake me with the news, I'd just have to wake him with it.

Once again the house was deathly quiet, but this time the silence felt good. I padded shoeless along the hall toward Jeff's room, first making sure Brent's door was closed. He should be the only other one left upstairs.

I'd intended to knock softly on Jeff's door before walking in, but it turned out not to be necessary. The door stood open, just like the closet door inside. Open and empty, room and closet alike. I stood there for a moment, not understanding, not wanting to understand. The police were finally gone, but so was the man I'd known as Jeff Allyn.

Chapter Fourteen

There was a small breakfast buffet put out by the time I got downstairs, but I ignored it in favor of the phone in the study. It was still raining, but the airport said its flights were still leaving, with only minor delays. There were two flights going to D.C., one later that morning and one in the afternoon, so I booked myself on both. I was determined to make at least one of them, even if I had to walk into town.

I left the desk and headed back toward the dining room, still working very hard not to think. If Jeff had left so abruptly during the night, it could only be because he'd been recalled. The ones trying to trap Carrie Tappan had themselves been trapped, and in any event I could be expected to handle things alone from here.

But not even a single word of goodbye? I paused with my hand on the doorknob, for the thousandth time wishing I knew whose fault that was. Had the man calling himself Jeff Allyn been playing a game with an available female, or had his people refused to allow him a final word with a woman he cared about?

Something had started to grow between us, I knew it had—but did he know it, too?

I took a deep breath and let it out slowly, coming to an unpleasant conclusion. If it had been me I would have stopped to say goodbye, no matter how unhappy it made Miller Houston. Had Jeff decided the point wasn't important enough to fight the government over? I understood that rules were stricter when they came from an official source, but even so...

Even so, I couldn't help thinking that Jeff had chosen his job over me. Intellectually I understood that, but emotionally I wasn't making it. I was silly enough to believe that if you really love someone, *nothing* is more important. But if that was the way he wanted it, trying to argue would be a waste of time. Besides, I had a job of my own to go back to.

Finally opening the door into the dining room showed me Brent standing at the buffet, and when he turned to see me he grinned.

"Hey, another familiar face!" he exclaimed. "I was beginning to think I was the only one left in the house. Have you had breakfast yet? And where's Jeff?"

"No, I haven't had breakfast," I answered as I walked toward him. "I was in there calling the airport, and learned that we can get flights out if we can find a way to get to the airport. I'm already packed, so all I need now is a ride."

"Maybe the cops left behind to keep an eye on us can arrange something," Brent suggested. "If they can I'll be packed in five minutes. But let's eat before we ask. Afterward we may not have the time."

It was a sensible suggestion, even if I didn't feel much like eating. I took some scrambled eggs and ham, a buttered roll and coffee, then followed Brent to the table. Three places had been set, which decreased my appetite even more.

For that final meal I sat at the head of the table, with Brent to my right. We finished most of our food in silence, then he leaned back to study me.

"You know he's gone, don't you," he said, and it was clear he was talking about Jeff. "Someone said there were higher-ups who wanted a more complete statement from him, so they took him into New Orleans. Why they also took his clothes I don't know, but they're definitely gone. I expect he'll go home rather than come back here."

I also leaned back to do some studying of my own, in no mood to play shy and backward. Brent's expression was sober and concerned, and that annoyed me.

"If you already knew all that," I said, "why did you ask me where he was when you first saw me? And what difference should it make to you *where* he goes?"

"Carrie, it wasn't me I was thinking about," he returned with gentle hurt in his voice. "I know you thought there was something developing between you and Jeff, but he's not the sort you can depend on. I'm really sorry you had to be disappointed this way, and if it makes you feel better to strike out at me, go right ahead. I don't mind in the least."

He reached over then to put his hand on mine, but I shifted it away before he could touch me.

"I'm sorry to have to tell you this, Brent, but you're not as good as you think you are," I remarked. "You can't put me on the defensive by playing the innocent martyr, and I won't be crying on your shoulder. You were trying to take advantage of me during what you thought was a vulnerable moment, and that's disgusting. As a human being, you'd make a good snake."

"Carrie, I don't understand what you're saying," he protested, still playing the game. "The only thing I was trying was to help, because I care. Why you're attacking me like that—"

"But didn't you say I could?" I interrupted with raised brows. "You invited me to strike out at you, expecting me to feel immediately guilty and apologize. Then you'd move in with the shoulder I could cry on, and eventually we'd notice we were just about alone in the house. I was also supposed to remember you'd warned me not to get involved with you, which was calculated to make me believe you were a decent person. Too bad, cousin, but none of it's going to work."

"Don't flatter yourself," he growled, his face red with embarrassment. "You're not so special that I would bother, not when there are women around who are *really* pretty. When you think things over and realize you've made a fool of yourself, forget about apologizing. I'll be too busy regretting trying to be your friend to listen."

He got up and left the table then, probably heading back to his room. If there was one thing to say about Brent, it was that he was persistent. His only problem was that his strategy was aimed at Carrie Tappan, who probably *would* have regretted saying all those nasty things to him. She would remember how unattractive she was, felt sorry about rejecting his friendship, then would have tried to apologize after all. What *I* did was shake my head in contempt, then refill my coffee cup.

The amount of food and extra flatware on the buffet led me to hope that the police were also expected for breakfast. For that reason I sat with my second cup of coffee and waited, and thankfully wasn't disappointed. The front door opened and two deputies in raincoats appeared in the dining room. They said they would be glad to give me a ride to the airport after they'd eaten; it was one of the reasons they'd been left there. I thanked them and went up to my room, made sure everything was packed, then carried the bags downstairs. It would be a short while before the deputies were ready, but impatience refused to let me sit still.

I was able to make the earlier flight out, and when I landed at Dulles I claimed my luggage and went straight home. Miller had wanted me to call him from the airport in New Orleans, but I didn't even call from Dulles or my apartment. I'd decided that what *I* wanted was thinking time, to ask and answer a few very pointed questions. One of them was whether or not to try competing with a federal agency.

When I finally reached the office, I was surprised to find it the same. After the past few days, it felt as if the entire world should be changed. There were no people there, of course, not on Saturday, but Miller made a habit of coming in on Saturday. I'd changed into my own clothes, a bright rose shirt and black stretch pants, along with black tennis shoes. The clothes were meant to take the taste of Carrie Tappan out of my mouth, the tennis shoes to show Miller I was serious about the vacation.

There was a note on my desk telling me to go to Miller's office as soon as I got in, so he knew I was back. It should have surprised me, but it didn't. Miller usually knew whatever he had to, and probably always would.

A knock on his door produced an invitation to come in, and when I did I *was* surprised. William Evans, the Tappans' lawyer, sat in one of the chairs in front of Miller's desk. Both men smiled at me as I took a chair, but Evans spoke first.

"I'm here, Ms. Mellion, to personally offer my congratulations on a job well done," he said. "I'll admit I had my reservations when Mrs. Tappan insisted on sending you in Carrie's place, but now I'm delighted that she did. Judge Mansard had the Louisiana authorities contact me with the details of what happened, and I've passed them on to Mr. Houston."

"And I had a friend of mine do some checking down there," Miller added. "The man calling himself James Nolan made a full confession, naming names and implicating some interesting foreign associates."

"One of them being an important client of mine," Evans supplied angrily. "Or perhaps I should say former client. I took Nolan on because they asked it as a favor, but when he became the only one I was able to send to Louisiana with you, I didn't care to extend the favor. That's why I never told him you weren't the real Carrie Tappan, and you have no idea how pleased I am that I didn't."

"I'm sure you know by now that they wanted Carrie as a lever against her father," Miller said to me, giving Evans a chance to cool off. "Everyone expected him to accept a post in London, and certain foreign powers saw a way to influence key actions in both our countries. An important message delivered wrong, or late, or not at all, for example, or slighting someone on purpose—Carrie's continued well-being would have depended on Tappan's full cooperation, and her life on his silence."

"Which would probably have been a pity," Evans put in, no longer looking pleased. "My client is a man with an incredibly strong sense of duty who puts it ahead of everything, including his family. If Carrie had been taken, he might well have sacrificed her to keep from being compromised."

"Nice man," I commented. "I'm delighted our country is represented by someone who would willingly throw his only child to the wolves. I envy Carrie's affluent life—I really do."

Neither man seemed to have an answer to that comment, or if they did they weren't given the time to make it. The door to Miller's office opened suddenly, and Eleanor Tappan hurried in. She left the door open behind her, but didn't seem to notice.

"One of you had better do something about this, and I mean immediately!" she commanded even before she reached us. "Everything was fine before this—this, incident!"

"Mrs. Tappan, calm yourself," Miller told her gently, standing to gesture to the chair on William Evans's left. "Please, sit down and tell us what's wrong."

"Everything's wrong," she stated, but still walked to the chair and sat stiffly. "Carrie has packed up and left. I want you to go to the place she and that—*creature* are living and bring her back."

"What creature?" Miller asked, still keeping his tone soothing. "Do you mean she's moved in with a man?"

"Heaven forbid!" Mrs. Tappan said sharply, looking completely outraged. "She hasn't done anything *that* disgusting. It's a girl she met at finishing school. The girl was obviously not the kind we wanted to know, and I told Carrie that at the time. She was not to have anything to do with someone who would never be a true lady. And then the girl was expelled. For totally unacceptable behavior, you understand, and I was delighted to know she was gone. I had no idea Carrie knew where she'd gone *to.*"

"Eleanor, you're still not telling us what happened," Evans put in, making his own attempt at soothing. "Take a deep breath and then start from the beginning."

"I don't need a deep breath," the woman responded, giving him a regal glance before returning her attention to Miller. "What I need is for one of you to bring my daughter to her senses. It all began yesterday, when my husband called from London. He'd been in meetings all week about which new post he would accept, and he'd narrowed the choice to England and Turkey. Naturally I told him Turkey was completely unacceptable, and it had to be England."

"Of course," Miller murmured, leaning back in his chair. "England is civilized, whereas Turkey is..."

"Completely unacceptable, exactly," Mrs. Tappan finished when he didn't, obviously thinking he agreed. "If I have to give up my lovely house here, it will be for the embassy in London, not in some backward place most people have never heard of. I told him so in no uncertain terms, and when we hung up I discovered that Carrie had overheard my part of the conversation."

"The argument disturbed her?" Miller asked. "Well, that would be the natural reaction of any child—"

"It was not an argument," Mrs. Tappan corrected immediately. "Ambassador Tappan and I are not common street people. We simply discuss matters between us, as civilized human beings should. What disturbed Carrie was the idea of moving to London. The silly child claimed she didn't like London, and actually tried to suggest that she remain in the house alone when her father and I left."

"Which you immediately refused to consider," I said, deciding it was time I participated. "If she stayed behind, she'd be out of your reach."

"And *in* the reach of every exploiter and user in the District," she agreed, clearly misinterpreting my meaning. "I didn't raise that child just to abandon her now, so of course I refused. I told her I didn't care to hear another word on the subject, and she obeyed me as usual. I considered the matter closed, and went about my usual business.

"This morning I had an executive board breakfast of my charity committee, a rather important one. One of our usual recipients was getting assistance from another group as well, and many of the ladies felt that lessened the appreciation we were due for our efforts. Well, the wrangling was intense, and what with one thing and another I didn't return home until about an hour ago. I went straight to Carrie's room to be certain she'd had her lunch—she'd skip meals if I allowed it—and that's when I found this note."

She fumbled in her purse for a moment, then produced a piece of cream-colored paper that had been folded in half. Miller was the one she handed it to, and he unfolded and scanned it before clearing his throat and starting to read.

> "Dear Mother, I know you love London, but I've hated every trip we ever made there. Even if Father chooses Turkey instead, as he probably will since that's where he feels he's needed most, I'll still hate being out of this country. It's finally been brought home to me that people can't make me do what I don't want to if I don't let them. I've therefore decided to move in with Jane Randolph, something she's suggested on and off for the past year or more. Please don't try to make me change my mind. It's time I began to make my own decisions about what's best for me, just as Jane has always said. Please give my regards to Father."

He paused and looked up, "Then she simply signed her name."

"You see?" Mrs. Tappan demanded. "The child has lost her mind, and it's all that Randolph creature's fault. I made a few telephone calls before coming here, and learned that the creature has turned her back on her own family. She lives in an apartment in a very common suburb, and actually has a job. My daughter has no business being in a place like that, and I want you to bring her home at once. I can't imagine why she would think she doesn't like London, but of course she's wrong. Everyone likes London, and as soon as she returns to her senses she'll remember that."

"Mrs. Tappan, how old is Carrie?" Miller asked gently, handing back the letter. "Isn't she a few months past twenty?"

"That's right," she answered with a nod. "Much too young to be off on her own, facing heaven knows what. That's why I—"

"Mrs. Tappan, the law doesn't agree with you," Miller said. "Once Carrie became eighteen, she was entitled to go and do as she pleased. You can check the point with Mr. Evans, who's luckily right here to be consulted. He—"

"Luck had nothing to do with it," the woman all but snapped. "I called his home first and learned that he was here. Conveniently so, as it turns out, since you don't seem capable of understanding plain English. I don't care what some silly law says. I want you to bring my daughter back home just as fast as is humanly possible. Tell him, William, and then agree to whatever fee he asks."

"Eleanor, stop talking and try listening," Evans said, his tone hard enough to draw her startled gaze. "Taking someone from where they want to be and bringing them to where they *don't* want to be is called kidnapping. You have no legal say over Carrie, and doing as you demand would probably get us all locked up. The girl has finally broken loose from you, and you'd be best advised to accept that."

"How dare you!" she snapped, glaring at him in outrage. "How dare you suggest that my daughter had to 'break loose,' as though I'd been holding her captive? She's my own flesh and blood, and I love her as much as any mother has ever loved a child. It's *her* welfare I'm concerned with, *her* safety and happiness! It's what a parent does when they love their child."

"No, it isn't," I disagreed when it was clear neither Evans nor Miller would challenge her statement. "If it was her you were thinking about, you wouldn't be here trying to get us to drag her back to you. Parents who really care *support* a child's first step out into the world, even if they're not sure the child is ready."

"What would *you* know about it?" she demanded with a cold up-and-down look at me. "How many children do *you* have that you can afford to criticize someone with experience?"

"You don't have to *have* children if you're close enough to remembering your own experience as one," I pointed out. "My parents are in love with Rome, but when I said I thought ruins grew very boring very fast, they didn't argue. They did *not* tell me everyone in the world loves Rome so I should too, nor did they say I had to love it because they did. They accepted my opinion as coming from someone entitled to have one. When have you ever done something like that for Carrie?"

"I'm sure your parents are wonderful examples, Ms. Mellion," she told me with a frosty smile. "They see Rome on a three-day package tour, then graciously accept the opinion of someone who hasn't even had that much exposure to it? How delightfully democratic of them."

"You really should stop assuming things, Mrs. Tappan," I said with a much warmer smile. "My parents are archaeologists who both have their doctorates, and Rome is where they stay between digs when there isn't enough time for them to come home. My sister and I would join them there whenever school vacations coincided, but these past few years we've both been too busy. Happily so, since my sister doesn't like Rome, either. But *our* mother never tried to tell us how to think."

"Then *your* mother is the one who's wrong," she growled. "When I was a girl my mother was always there to show me where I was wrong, to teach me the right way things should be done. If she hadn't people would have laughed and pointed at me, or at the very least smiled behind their hands. She kept me from making a fool of myself, and I've always been grateful. Carrie is grateful to *me,* and I want her back!"

"Carrie is smothered by you, and she doesn't want to *be* back," I ground out. "What bothers you most, I think, is that she's had the courage to do something you never did. You've lost, Mrs. Tappan, and it's time you admitted it."

"That isn't true," she whispered, her light skin now ashen. "Children usually don't know what's right—that's why they need parents. To show them the proper, to teach them the acceptable. If I'd ignored my duty, she would have ruined her life."

"Please save the excuses," I said with a gesture of weariness, but refusing to let up on the pressure. "Children need to be taught the basics, but after that need most to be taught how to make their own decisions. *That's* a parent's first duty—to make the child they raise a mature, capable adult. If you didn't do that for your own child, and you certainly didn't, don't you dare use the word 'duty.'"

"Tommy, aren't you being somewhat hard on Mrs. Tappan?" Miller put in, trying to smooth things over. "She did what she thought best, after all."

"Garbage," I said distinctly. "That's another excuse people like to comfort themselves with, and it doesn't wash. Opinions don't count, only results do. If your child is confident and knows your support can be counted on in a crisis, you've done it right. If your child is constantly straining against the apron strings—or worse, doesn't even realize they're there—you haven't. Was Carrie taught to face life on her own and handle it herself? The answer to that is the answer to whether or not this woman was a good parent."

Rather than saying anything else, Mrs. Tappan was suddenly on her feet and heading for the door. We all watched her go in silence, but I couldn't help feeling she'd be back to her old self by the next day at the latest.

"At least one good thing came out of this," William Evans said with a sigh once his client was gone. "Carrie will have enough money to support herself until she learns something useful. Eleanor will be lucky if the girl ever wants to see her again."

"That's the price you pay when you run your child's life to suit yourself rather than the child," Miller said, surprising me. "Carrie is lucky in another way, as well. Very soon her mother will be too busy getting ready to leave the country to bother her much."

"To go to England, you mean?" Evans asked. "I understand the decision still has to be made, which could take days or weeks."

"The decision was made today," Miller replied with a faint smile. "The papers should have it by tonight, so I'm not telling tales out of school. Our country has a new ambassador to Turkey."

"Oh, dear," Evans said, looking startled. "Carrie was right, and Eleanor will be devastated. But if a threat to Carrie's life wouldn't have swayed the man, Eleanor's preferences probably went totally unconsidered."

"And that man had the nerve to claim family matters were important to him," Miller commented. "He probably said it only because the stance is politically proper, but he'll regret his real attitude if he lives long enough. Caring more about work than you do about your family leads to a very lonely old age."

Miller was almost thinking out loud, and had managed to surprise me for the second time. Evans nodded broodingly, as though he'd learned the same point. Then he came out of it and stood, saying it was time he was on his way.

"We really appreciate your coming by," Miller said, leaving his chair to offer his hand as he walked Evans to the door. "And thank you again for your decision to recommend us to your clients and associates. We won't disappoint your faith in us."

Evans murmured something about being sure we wouldn't, then he was gone and the door was closed behind him. Miller came back to his desk and sat, studied me for a moment, then shook his head.

"I'm not even going to *think* about the possibility that it's your fault as well that the girl left home," he said at last. "If her mother ever finds out it is— When are you going to learn not to mind other people's business?"

"When I stop living in this world," I answered, strangely unworried about his anger. "And I'm *not* responsible for Carrie's leaving. That's a decision only the person involved can be responsible for."

"Something's bothering you," Miller observed, his eyes narrowed. "Did something happen in Louisiana that I don't know about yet? When I found out what flight you were on, I expected you to at least call me from Dulles. Why didn't you?"

"I didn't because I preferred saying this in person," I told him, wishing I'd gotten a cup of coffee before coming to his office. "All career aspirations aside, I need that vacation you've been dangling in front of me. Since I need it now, I also need your answer. Do I get it or not?"

"Something did happen," he stated, now looking worried. "I know an ultimatum when I hear one, and I never expected to hear it from you. If I don't give you a vacation, you'll quit."

"Please save the grim drama," I told him with a sigh. "I've more than earned a vacation, and I'm not in the mood to play word games. If you want to think of yourself as the innocent victim of blackmail, go right ahead. That won't change the fact that Monday I won't be here. Whether I'm on vacation or permanently gone is your decision—which I'd appreciate having in the next hour or so. I'll be in my office, dictating my report on the Tappan business."

I got up and headed for the door, but didn't get more than a few steps. His quiet "Ann" stopped me, a seriousness to his voice that I'd never heard before.

"Ann, you *have* more than earned a vacation," he said, his dark gaze directly on my face. "I don't know how you'll be spending it, but if I can help in any way just let me know. When you're ready to come back, we'll find something else to advance your career."

He smiled then, an encouraging smile that said I really was important to him. No prying questions, no more demands to know what had happened, only support and a reminder that he was there if I needed him. Just the reaction I would have expected from my father—my real father. My question about Miller had been answered, and in the very best way possible. I returned his smile with a nod, and then I continued on out.

I stopped for that cup of coffee on the way back to my office, sorry that Marsha wasn't there. I wanted to tell her that I'd decided the right man was more important than the right job. For some women that didn't apply but for me it did, and I knew Marsha would understand. Starting the next day I would be tracking down the man I'd known as Jeff Allyn. If he really had more interest in his work than in me, I wanted him to tell me so to my face.

I was three strides into my office before I noticed what was on my desk—something that almost made me drop the coffee. A fairly large gift-wrapped box sat where there had been no box before, and a card jutted from one corner. It must have been brought by the downstairs building guard while I was in Miller's office.

Half of me wanted to run to see what the card said, but the other half understood that sometimes gifts were sent with goodbyes. I compromised by walking slowly to the desk, putting the coffee down, then lifting the top from the box. If it turned out to be some sort of joke...

But it wasn't. Some magic had told me who the box was from, and where magic works it doesn't lie. Inside the box was a bouquet made up of Dr. Pepper bottles, with a pretty pink ribbon tying them together. I laughed a little with the most wonderful premonition, then grabbed for the card.

"Now I can't *forget,"* it read. *"How about you?"*

I read it three or four times, wishing he were there to get my answer in person. I'd already decided to try to find him, but what if I hadn't? What if I'd simply walked away without waiting to hear a final goodbye from him?

"Well?" I heard a voice say. "Don't you believe in answering questions put to you?"

It was him, leaning against the doorjamb as he watched me. I tossed the card onto the desk, heading for the real thing, and he met me halfway. His arms were delicious and his kiss took my breath away, but who needs breath? I had what I needed, and when the kiss ended I couldn't keep from laughing.

"What's so funny?" he asked, looking the tiniest bit hurt. "If you plan on doing that every time I kiss you, it will very likely become a problem."

"I was just picturing my next conversation with my parents," I answered, hugging him tighter. "Mom and Dad, I'll say, I just met the most wonderful man. What's his name? Uh, I can't tell you that. What does he do for a living? Well, I can't tell you that, either. They'll be back in this country so fast, Customs won't recover for a month."

"As long as you can tell them you love me," he said with a grin matching mine. "Not to mention the fact that I also love you. I've been announcing that to people since last night, and I think they finally believe me. Which they'd better. I wasn't joking about anything I said."

"I had a feeling leaving like that wasn't your idea," I said, stroking his back. "Or at least I was hoping it wasn't. What happened?"

"They got me out of the house by pretending to be from the local D.A.'s office," he said, anger in his eyes at the memory. "They talked about debriefing me, but instead of doing it in New Orleans, they stuffed me on a family jet. I was back here almost before I knew it, and then they decided that since I was here I might as well stay here."

"I don't think I would have enjoyed being the one to tell you that," I said with a faint smile. "Was it the agency you were on loan to, or your own people?"

"My people weren't involved until I got them involved," he said, stroking my hair. "I told them how things stood between us, then gave them a choice. They could either have the directive against associating with you revoked, or they could have my resignation. The decision was entirely theirs."

"And they decided to let you go ahead and date?" I asked. "That was really nice of them, but what if next time you ask for more? Will they send you to summer camp to give you a chance to forget me?"

"They haven't decided anything yet," he said with a shake of his head. "As soon as I told them how *I* saw it, I went out to get that bouquet for you. I wanted to be here when you got back, but there was confusion about which flight you'd be on. When I finally found out you'd taken the earlier flight, it was too late to meet you or even to be here first. And Tommy, I didn't say a word about dating. I had something a bit more permanent in mind—even if I end up unemployed. If worse comes to worst, I can always ask *you* for a job."

We both laughed at that, then we shared another kiss. I didn't mention that I'd almost ended up unemployed myself, because it wouldn't have mattered even if I had. We'd make things work out one way or another, whether they took him back or not. As long as we were together, everything would be fine.

"Ann, about that report," I heard, then hurriedly moved away from Jeff. Miller had started into my office, but then had stopped short with his brows raised. "Excuse me. I didn't realize you had a visitor. Under the circumstances, I think I'd like to be introduced to the gentleman."

I didn't believe I was actually blushing, but Miller was looking so parentally stern that I couldn't help it. And he wanted to be introduced! I couldn't introduce Jeff as Jeff, not when he *wasn't* Jeff anymore. I stood there like an idiot, trying to think of something to say, and a broad arm circled my shoulders.

"I'm Steve Jensen, sir, and you must be Miller Houston," Jeff said smoothly as he put his hand out. "Ann has told me so much about you that I've looked forward to meeting you in person. Do you realize you're a legend in this town?"

"Now, now, none of that," Miller scolded, but he was also smiling and taking the hand being offered. He was sometimes willing to be flattered, but only if the flatterer did it right. Apparently Jeff was doing it right—or Steve was. Could that be his real name? If not, what *was* his name?

Then the arm around me tightened, and I realized I didn't care. The man of my dreams had come alive, and life didn't get much better than that.

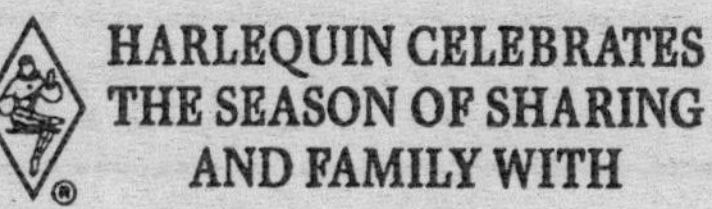

Harlequin introduces the latest member in its family of seasonal collections. Following in the footsteps of the popular *My Valentine, Just Married* and *Harlequin Historical Christmas Stories,* we are proud to present FRIENDS, FAMILIES, LOVERS. A collection of three new contemporary romance stories about America at its best, about welcoming others into the circle of love.... Stories to warm your heart...

By three leading romance authors:

KATHLEEN EAGLE
SANDRA KITT
RUTH JEAN DALE

Available in October, wherever Harlequin books are sold.

THANKS